THEY CAME TO CHEYENNE

Caroline Wells—A beautiful woman and a more-than-capable rancher, she has come to Cheyenne to bring her wastrel of a brother home before her father dies.

Kyle Warner—Years ago, he made a blood pact with the Apache chieftain who saved his life. Now he will risk everything to return the favor.

Mary Beth Smith—She had to summon all of her courage to flee her fearful past. But in Cheyenne, she will be forced to make her most trying decision.

Santoro—A proud, powerful Apache, he has been falsely accused of murder—and only his bold blood brother can save him.

Captain Bill Farnum—Charged with maintaining law and order in the West, he will stop at nothing to bring Santoro to military justice.

D1308119

The Stagecoach Series
Ask your bookseller for the books you have missed

STAGECOACH STATION 3:

CHEYENNE

Hank Mitchum

 Created by the producers of
**Wagons West, White Indian,
Saga of the Southwest,** and
The Kent Family Chronicles Series.

Executive Producer: Lyle Kenyon Engel

BANTAM BOOKS

TORONTO · NEW YORK · LONDON · SYDNEY · AUCKLAND

CHEYENNE

*A Bantam Book / published by arrangement with
Book Creations, Inc.*

Bantam edition / December 1982

2nd printing ... December 1982	4th printing .... June 1983
3rd printing ...... March 1983	5th printing .... February 1984
6th printing . . . April 1985	

*Produced by Book Creations, Inc.
Chairman of the Board: Lyle Kenyon Engel.*

ISBN 0-553-24015-3

Published simultaneously in the United States and Canada

PRINTED IN THE UNITED STATES OF AMERICA

O   15   14   13   12   11   10   9   8   7   6

STAGECOACH STATION 3:

CHEYENNE

Chapter 1

It was early, a few minutes after seven on a clear morning late in August of 1868. The Wells Fargo stage was almost ready to pull out of Fort Laramie, Wyoming Territory, on the final leg of its journey to Cheyenne, one hundred miles to the south. A small but growing crowd of spectators had gathered as usual to watch the preparations. In this remote country, where the railroad's coming was only a rumor as yet, the magnificent Concord coach in front of the express office was still a sight to behold.

Eight feet tall and weighing more than a ton, the coach could accommodate as many as twenty-one passengers; there were three upholstered benches inside that held nine passengers, and room for a dozen more on the roof. Admired throughout the West for its speed, splendor, and extraordinary durability, the Concord's running gear, fashioned of elm, oak, and hickory, was so solid and durable that Tim Moody—its present Jehu, or driver—swore that it would outlast the ironwork.

During its long trip from Billings, Montana Territory, the coach had acquired a heavy patina of dust and grime. Nevertheless, the Concord's basswood side panels remained a gleaming red, and some of the brightest features of the landscape that had been painted on it could still be discerned by those in the crowd who were close enough.

1

As the hostler finished hitching up the four-horse team—six horses would be used for a heavier load—Tim Moody emerged from the express office and looked across the street at the Fort Laramie Hotel. He had already sent word to the desk clerk that he was pulling out in less than fifteen minutes, yet only a few of his passengers were visible on the hotel's front porch.

With a shrug of his powerful shoulders, the big man descended the express-office steps and headed for his coach to wait for Seth, his express messenger, to bring out the gold shipment they would be carrying to Cheyenne. The two of them had spent a long night guarding the two chests, and Moody wanted no hitch now in bringing them out.

As soon as Caroline Wells saw the driver head for the stagecoach, she stepped through the hotel doorway to join the other passengers on the porch.

She was a tall, slender woman of twenty-three. Her auburn curls coiled thickly down her shoulders, their luster a perfect match for the piercing, uncompromising eyes that flashed out from under her broad eyebrows. She wore no rouge, since her high cheekbones and full lips needed no such embellishment.

Dressed for travel, she was wearing a wasp-waisted, mint-green corduroy dress, with lace at her throat and wrists. On her head she wore a straw boater with a small yellow feather in its brim, and on her feet, black, high-topped shoes. Though it was obvious from the casual way she held herself that she did not take easily to this formal style of dress, she looked splendid, nevertheless. As she strode out onto the porch, two townsmen conversing near the entrance found themselves unable to keep their eyes off her.

Caroline's luggage had already been loaded onto the coach by the hotel bellhop. Another grueling ride lay ahead of her. At times during her trip from Billings, the queasy sway of the coach rocking on its leather thorough-braces had made her afraid she might get sick. But she was no longer worried about that. It was the boredom, not the ceaseless rocking of the coach, that bothered her—a boredom that allowed her to dwell on the growing hopelessness she felt whenever she considered the ramifications of her desperate mission to Cheyenne.

A sharp cry caused her to turn quickly.

A man and a woman were struggling in the hotel doorway. Caroline knew the woman. Her name was Mary Beth Smith, and she was one of today's passengers for Cheyenne. Caroline had spoken to her briefly during break-fast. She had seemed quite nervous then, and now Caroline knew why.

The man had grabbed one of Mary Beth's wrists, and while Caroline watched in growing anger, he slapped her twice with brutal efficiency, snapping her head sharply around with each blow.

"Stop that!" Caroline cried, hurrying toward the struggling couple. "How dare you!"

The fellow flung the woman from him and turned on Caroline, his stubbled, dirty face distorted with rage. "Stay out of this, lady! It ain't none of your business. This here's my wife."

Caroline held up, appalled.

A few of the men on the porch behind Caroline began to mutter. But not one of them stepped forward to help Mary Beth, who was cowering now with her back against the doorjamb, her right hand held up to her cheek, tears coursing down her face. She looked so terrified and helpless that Caroline's heart went out to her.

"I don't care if Mary Beth *is* your wife," Caroline protested boldly, aware of the disapproving glances from the men watching. "That gives you no call to treat her like this!"

Mary Beth's husband laughed. It was a frightening sound. "Oh, don't it now," he retorted. "This here woman of mine done run away! She up and left me and her own son—that's what she done! She don't even care about her own boy! What kind of a woman would do such a thing as that? She says she's goin' home to her mother! Not likely! All the way East on the pennies she's squirreled away? She's got herself a man, that's what!"

In a fury now, Mary Beth's husband turned once more on his wife, grabbed her by the front of her dress, and began shaking her brutally.

"Who is he?" the man demanded. "Tell me! I want to know who you're meetin' in Cheyenne!"

Mary Beth tried to answer her husband, but the man was shaking her so violently that she couldn't get a word out. With a sudden, furious oath, the man flung her from him. Mary Beth struck the doorway, tried to grab hold of something, then stumbled backward and fell to the floor of the porch.

Striding closer, the man glared down at his wife. "You ain't goin' nowhere!" he snarled at her. "You're goin' home with me right now! Let's see that ticket!"

"No, Amos!" Mary Beth cried raggedly. "I won't give it to you! I'm leaving you!"

"No, you ain't, dammit!" Amos cried, reaching down and hauling the woman to her feet. "Didn't you hear what I just told you?"

Caroline forgot herself. Reaching over swiftly, she grabbed Amos's arm and attempted to restrain him. With a vicious oath, he cuffed Caroline out of his way, catching her on the side of the head. Her ears ringing, she almost lost her balance as she staggered back.

"All right there, mister," said a low, menacing voice just behind Caroline. "I suggest you step back away from both them women."

Caroline glanced around to see a thin, pale man dressed in black advancing on Mary Beth's husband—a gleaming, ivory-handled Smith & Wesson in his hand. He was a gambler, she knew—a drawn, wasted fellow, his eyes peering out from deep hollows, the hectic flush of the consumptive rouging his hollow cheeks.

Amos took one look at the weapon in the gambler's hand and quickly drew back. "Hey now, listen here, mister," he whined. "You got no call to go messin' in my private affairs. Didn't you hear me? This here woman's my wife."

"I heard," the gambler said laconically. "But that don't make me like what I'm seeing. A man may own the horse he's beating, but no one with any sand will stand by and let him do it."

"This here's a family matter! I'm warnin' you!"

The pale fellow smiled, his teeth gleaming like lightning in a cloud. "You can warn me all you want, mister. But I suggest you get off this porch and out of my sight. And do it sudden like. I'm getting tired of holding this iron on you. I might want to lighten it some."

Amos glanced swiftly, furiously at his wife. At once she cowered back fearfully, flinging her hands up to protect herself. "Mary Beth!" the man cried. "You comin' with me?"

"No!" she replied. "No! Leave me be!"

Amos spun around, brushed angrily past Caroline, and stalked off the porch. "You ain't heard the last of this, mister!" he cried up at the gambler as he reached the street. "And you, too, Mary Beth! I'll be after you. You just wait!"

He swiftly strode off.

Caroline, shuddering, watched him disappear, then turned around and hurried over to Mary Beth. As she put her arms around the woman to comfort her, Caroline looked at the gambler. He had holstered his revolver and was coughing softly into a handkerchief he was holding up to his mouth.

"Thank you, Mister...?"

"Dirk Taggart, ma'am," the man answered, carefully tucking his handkerchief back into his breast pocket. "Pleased to meet you. I trust that no-account's blow was not too serious."

"I'm fine, thank you," Caroline replied.

To escape the chill she felt when looking into the gambler's cold eyes, Caroline hurriedly turned back to Mary Beth.

"Thank you for helping me, Mr. Taggart," Mary Beth said, wiping away her tears. "But you should be careful. My husband is a very violent man."

"That was quite obvious, ma'am. But I am not worried, I assure you. Will you be all right now?"

"Yes, thank you."

"I'll stay with Mary Beth," Caroline told Taggart. "But we must hurry. The stage is ready to go."

As she spoke, she pulled Mary Beth away from him toward the porch steps. Taggart smiled and bowed slightly. Again, Caroline felt the chill in his smile and looked away. Though Taggart had helped them, it was obvious that he was a man accustomed to violence, a man more than casually familiar with violent death.

Louise Thompson had watched the entire episode,

noting with contempt the way every man but Dirk Taggart had kept his distance while that cad named Amos struck at his wife. Now she moved up beside Taggart and smiled boldly at him.

"It appears there ain't too many men around here big enough to protect a woman," she told him.

Taggart smiled and bowed gallantly. "Perhaps. At any rate, I was glad to be of some service."

Taggart had noticed this woman at dinner the night before. She had impressed him then and she impressed him now. A handsome woman in her early forties, her auburn curls were streaked with gray. But a masterly application of rouge and powder and the discipline it took to keep her lush figure within bounds had done much to deny those years.

The revealing, saucy cut of her neckline and the vivid, satiny sheen of her red velvet dress were a frank admission that her profession was the world's oldest. But, like Taggart, she made no effort to hide who or what she was. A blunt, outspoken honesty obviously governed her every action. And at the moment she was not at all reluctant to meet Taggart's bold glance with one of her own.

"My name's Louise Thompson," she told him. "I'm on my way to Cheyenne."

"Dirk Taggart, ma'am. Pleased to meet you. I, too, am on my way to Cheyenne. Shall we make for the coach together, Louise?"

As he spoke, he gave her his arm. She took it, and together they descended the porch steps and headed for the coach.

Across the street—unmindful of the commotion that had just erupted on the hotel porch—Captain Bill Farnum of the Third Cavalry pushed his prisoner ahead of him toward the coach.

Ramrod straight, the captain was a graduate of West Point and proud of it. His eyes were an icy blue, his jaw solid and unyielding. Dressed neatly, almost meticulously, in full uniform, he walked just behind the prisoner, his implacable gaze intent on the man he had journeyed so long and so far to apprehend—the Apache chieftain, Santoro.

The fact that Farnum had an Apache captive drew a crowd at once—just as it had the night before, when he had marched the Indian off to the stockade. Now, a few in the crowd behind the captain shouted out repeatedly, declaring that there was no need to take the Apache prisoner south to New Mexico for justice. The entire matter, they insisted, could all be handled just as neatly here in Fort Laramie.

Ignoring the cries, Farnum stepped off the boardwalk and approached the coach with his prisoner. As he did, a tall, rangy rancher in a buckskin jacket approached from across the street. For an instant the captain had the odd impression that the fellow intended to interfere with him and his prisoner. Instead, the man veered off and walked on past them, his eyes resting only momentarily on the Apache. Farnum reached the stage, pulled the door open for his manacled prisoner, then shoved the Indian into the coach ahead of him.

As Santoro sat down in the rear seat, he swiftly glanced out past the rolled-up leather curtain, his eyes searching for the tall fellow in the buckskin jacket. He found him standing on the edge of the boardwalk, looking intently at the stagecoach. Their eyes met once again. For just an instant, the Indian's craggy, powerful face lit. Then the old warrior looked back at his fellow passengers, the cold mask of his face once more impenetrable.

*　　*　　*

The tall rancher in the buckskin jacket was Kyle Warner. He was wearing Levi's, scuffed riding boots, and a black, flat-crowned plainsman's hat. On his right hip a Colt .44 rode in an open, flapless holster. Over six feet tall, almost gaunt in his leanness, he had a strong nose, a square, cleft chin, high cheekbones, and piercing, steel-gray eyes.

They were narrowed now in concern as Kyle watched Santoro settle back into his seat. Kyle had wanted the Apache to know that he was aware of his blood brother's capture—and would do what he could to effect his escape. It was vital that the old Apache not lose hope and as a result do something foolish. Kyle knew what fetters or imprisonment of any kind did to an Indian, especially an Apache.

Someone nudged Kyle to one side. Stepping back, Kyle turned to see a wide-eyed storekeeper push past to get closer to the edge of the boardwalk. He was holding a fresh coil of rope in his hand.

"Leave that Injun here!" the fellow brayed. "I've got a fresh rope here needs stretchin'!"

A roar of approval went up all around Kyle, but there was no response from the stagecoach.

All six of its passengers were inside by this time, and the Jehu was climbing up onto his lordly perch. The young express messenger, a double-barreled shotgun in his hand, had just pulled open the side door of the coach and was busy inspecting the mail sacks and other baggage that had been piled on the floor beneath the center bench. Earlier, Kyle had watched as the Jehu, the express messenger, and three other express clerks had manhandled two chests of gold up into the boot under the driver's seat.

Satisfied, the express messenger slammed shut the

door of the coach and climbed up beside the driver. As soon as he was settled, the Jehu clapped his reins over the backs of his four horses and let loose with a thunderous, "*Yahh!*"

At once the horses started up, their shoes digging frantically into the dry ground. The coach lurched forward, rocking on its thoroughbraces, then rattled away from the express office, gaining speed with each second. The Jehu went to his bullwhip then and sent it snaking out over the horses' backs. He cracked it once, twice. The team settled into a gallop, and in a moment the stage was on its way out of town, a cloud of dust spinning slowly behind it.

The crowd broke up. It was still early, and for most who had been watching, a day of hard, interminable work stretched before them. Still talking excitedly among themselves, they moved off down the street. For a short while this morning, the stagecoach had been their theater, and even more—an exciting reminder that they might also travel to distant cities, perhaps even to foreign lands, someday. But for now they were left in the dust of the departing stage, confronted once again with the dull reality of their tiny outpost here in Wyoming Territory.

Watching the townsmen move off, Kyle felt little sympathy for them or for their cramped lives. Just a few moments before, in their eagerness to hang a fellow human being, they had revealed the yawning emptiness, the aridity of their white hearts. If their lives were dull, Kyle was certain it was their mean souls that made it so.

Hurrying on down the walk, Kyle opened a livery-stable door. Inside, three men were waiting beside four saddled horses. Kyle did not like having to deal with such human offal, but the way he saw it, he had no choice. Not if he was going to achieve Santoro's freedom.

The three men were brothers—the Donner brothers.

10

The tallest and eldest was Will. Luke and Flem were both smaller and, to Kyle's mind, meaner. They still stank of the whiskey Kyle had plied them with the night before in his effort to convince them that he should be allowed to join their robbery of the Cheyenne stage.

Now, as the three brothers blearily glared at him through bloodshot eyes, Kyle realized they were no longer so certain he should be allowed to throw in with them.

"The gold's on board," he told them, ignoring the hostility in their eyes. "Two boxes containing solid gold bars. We'll need a mule to carry it off, I'm thinking."

"We'll do without a mule," Will Donner said, wiping his nose with a filthy sleeve. "We'll split up the haul after we get it—then light out. I suggest you go in a different direction from us, Warner."

"Yeah," said Luke, grinning. What few teeth he had left were yellow and as crooked as an old picket fence.

Will Donner looked at Kyle closely. "The only reason we're gonna let you tag along, Warner, is to keep you quiet. Guess you might say you ain't exactly welcome."

Kyle nodded as affably as he could under the circumstances. "I understand," he said. "But you won't regret it. If anything goes wrong, you'll be glad you've got my extra gun."

"There ain't nothin' gonna go wrong," Will replied evenly.

Flem Donner smiled. "It better not, is what Will means," the man told Kyle.

Flem was a slovenly hulk with a reddish stubble covering his face. His eyes were lit with a crazy meanness. Of all of them, Flem had been the most difficult for Kyle to convince the night before. He had been astonished at the prodigious amount of whiskey the man had consumed.

11

"Well, let's go, then," Kyle said. "We got a ride ahead of us."

He swung up onto his powerful roan gelding, clapped spurs to its flanks, and cantered out of the livery. The three brothers mounted up and rode out after him.

In a moment, with Kyle still in the lead, the four riders clattered out of Fort Laramie, the dust they raised almost as thick as that left by the Cheyenne stage only a few moments before.

Chapter 2

It was stifling inside the stagecoach. In order to withstand the ceaseless rocking motion of the coach, Caroline had braced her feet against the center bench as she stared out at the arid, midsummer landscape.

Beside her sat Mary Beth, her head resting against the seat, her eyes still swollen from the tears she had continued to shed for a long time after the stage had pulled out of Fort Laramie. She preferred to let Caroline think she was asleep, since she didn't want to cause any further concern. Caroline had been kind enough already. It was thoughts of her twelve-year-old son, Caleb, that tormented her. At times the ache was so great that she wanted to cry out. Could Amos be right about her? After all, what kind of woman must she be to be willing to abandon her own son?

Louise Thompson was sitting next to the window, beside Mary Beth. Directly across from her sat Dirk Taggart. The two were not able to say too much above the ceaseless rattle of the stage, but they managed to get acquainted, nevertheless, and after the noon sun began to cook them, they began passing back and forth a flask of whiskey. The result was that Taggart's pale death's-head of a face achieved some color, however faint, and Louise Thompson's voice became deeper and huskier, her occasional laugh a bit more hearty.

13

Wedged between Taggart and the captain sat the Apache. His face was expressionless, his dark eyes gleaming like wet coal. He seemed unaware of everyone else in the coach as he sat back rigidly in his seat. It was as if he had removed his consciousness from his human form and had simply gone elsewhere.

The manacles about Santoro's wrists were constructed of iron cuffs connected by a short length of chain secured by a padlock, the key to which the captain kept on a rawhide thong around his neck. After capturing him, Farnum had engaged the services of a blacksmith in the first town he reached. The manacles that had resulted were more than adequate.

As Santoro leaned back against the seat, he recalled the face of his blood brother. Just as he, Santoro, had protected Kyle Warner and his family from other Apache years ago, so now Kyle would free him from this stone heart of a captain. This was what Kyle's eyes had told him. It was for this reason that Santoro endured this prison on wheels and told himself not to leap upon any of his fellow passengers.

But despite the hope that Kyle Warner's face had stirred to life within him, Santoro still felt the manacles on his wrists as an intolerable weight on his soul. And deep within him, his imprisoned soul wept.

The captain, sitting across from Caroline Wells, did his best to keep himself as straight and unperturbed by the coach's ceaseless motion as was his captive. As a result, he found it difficult not to look into the young woman's cool, lovely face and marvelously dark eyes.

Once, not long out of Fort Laramie, she had met his gaze directly. Taken by surprise, he had felt himself blush and had quickly looked away—out past the dusty leather curtains at the rolling landscape. And that had been a poor substitute for her lovely face. Still, he had kept his gaze resolutely away from her disconcerting eyes, keeping his thoughts on the matter at hand.

And this was not easy, due to the scandalous behavior of the gambler and his woman. She was a prostitute—of that he had not the slightest doubt. And he was certain that her presence and behavior were a shock to Miss Wells and the Smith woman. He sighed inwardly, forcing his thoughts into other channels, and soon found himself recalling the potential lynch mob that had gathered around the stage at Fort Laramie.

He was proud that so far he had resisted and would continue to resist the demands of all those citizens who were so eager to take his captive from him and mete out their own form of rude justice. It was not frontier justice he wanted for this Apache renegade, but military justice: cold, correct, and final. In his escape from the reservation, Santoro and his band had massacred a settler and his family. And for that Farnum intended to see Santoro hang.

Watching the captain from her seat, Caroline could feel the man's intensity, his single-minded, obsessive need to bring this Apache to justice. She could also sense the suppressed desperation that filled the Indian, despite the emotionless expression on his powerful face.

For a moment, just before the stage pulled out, she had noticed a brief flicker of hope cross the Indian's face, after which the Apache had sunk back into his seat. She had no idea what could have given the old chieftain that momentary flash of hope, and she wondered about it.

Caroline took a deep breath and tried to relax, but she found it difficult. For some inexplicable reason, she had a feeling that all was not as it seemed, that trouble was afoot. It hung in the stifling air of the stagecoach like something tangible. That frightening scene she had witnessed between Mary Beth and her husband probably contributed to this feeling, serving as an omen, perhaps. Thinking back on how that ugly little man had dared to treat his wife made her shudder. Mary Beth's husband was little better than an animal. What in heaven's name could have possessed her to have married such a man in the first place?

And that thought brought her to Ted Smithers, the young rancher who wanted to marry her. As Caroline glanced out at the sunbaked landscape, she found herself going over in her mind her departure from Billings and Ted's unhappiness with her. It seemed almost impertinent of her to deny a man who was so obviously eligible. Everyone had thought their marriage was inevitable—everyone but her, that is.

On Caroline's departure, Ted had importuned her mercilessly, pleading with her to give him an answer before she left. She had felt his desperation and need, but nevertheless she had insisted on leaving without giving him her word. The sudden, petulant anger she had seen in his eyes had dismayed and disappointed her. At the same time, it had convinced her that her instincts were correct. She needed more time. She did not really trust Ted—or her feelings for him.

Her father, bless him, had told her as much, insisting that she need not make a decision until she was ready. Caroline wondered if it was her father's uncertainty about Ted that had caused her own doubts, for though he had never said anything, she could tell there was something about the young rancher that he did not entirely trust.

The moment Caroline thought of her father, a sharp ache closed about her heart. Three weeks earlier a stroke had cut him down. There was no doubt that her brother's disappearance had contributed to it. She had seen the foreshadowing change in her father from the moment when, almost a year ago, Silas Maskin rode in to break the news that Everett had withdrawn his share of the ranch's money from the bank and had ridden out.

What Everett was in search of, no one knew. Adventure, perhaps freedom from his father's domination. It did not matter, really. All that mattered to Caroline's father was that his son—his heir—was gone. Caroline had been standing on the veranda beside him when Silas rode up, and she had witnessed the effect the banker's words had on him. It was as if an invisible bolt of lightning had knifed out of the blue sky above them and cut through her father, instantly transforming him into an old man.

All that mattered now was that she find Everett and bring him back to her father before it was too late. The hope of seeing his prodigal son again was all that kept the man alive. She could still see the desperate hope that had filled his eyes the day she had left him with the promise to bring Everett back.

But would she succeed? First, she would have to find him. The West was huge. So much could have happened in the six months since Everett had last written her from Cheyenne. And even if she did find him, would she be able to convince him to come back? . . .

Captain Farnum's sharp voice cut into her thoughts. She quickly looked back at him and saw that he was speaking to Dirk Taggart. The gambler was holding his flask up to the Apache's face, offering him a drink.

"Put that away, mister!" the captain commanded for the second time. "I'm not going to tell you again."

"Hell, Captain. Ain't no harm in giving the poor fool a taste. It's as hot as the coffers of hell in here."

Ignoring the captain, Taggart said to the Apache, "Here, Injun. Have a little firewater!"

The Indian's impenetrable mask broke. There was a

flicker of appreciation in the man's magnificent dark eyes, and he began to raise his manacled hands to take the flask.

With an oath, Farnum reached swiftly across the Indian and slapped the flask away. Taggart almost lost his grip on the flask as whiskey spilled over his knees. Patiently, obviously restraining himself with great difficulty, the gambler took out his handkerchief and carefully wiped off his pants.

"You better not lay a hand on me again, Captain," Taggart said, his voice icy with menace. "I'm not some poor Indian you ran down—or some private in your ranks. You've got no authority over me."

"Perhaps not, mister," the captain replied evenly, "but I would remind you that selling spirits to Indians is against federal law—selling it *or* giving it away. Further, I feel I should also warn you that I heartily disapprove of the way you and this . . . painted hussy have been carrying on. You forget—there are two *decent* women in this coach, who are not amused by your behavior."

Caroline was shocked by the captain's words. Dirk Taggart was more than shocked. With the speed of a striking snake, his pale left hand reached out and slapped the captain, hard. At the same time, his revolver appeared in his right hand as if by magic.

"I'm waiting for your apology to the lady, mister," Taggart said, his face flushed. "But I don't plan to wait long."

"She has it, of course," Captain Farnum replied coolly. "I do not have much of an alternative at the moment. But if you wish, sir, I will be most anxious to give you satisfaction—in a more appropriate time and at a more appropriate place."

"Sure," drawled Taggart, holstering his weapon wearily, the cold fire draining from his face. "Anytime you say, Captain. You just be sure to remind me."

"You may rest assured I will."

Without responding to him, Taggart handed the flask to Louise Thompson. But she shook her head, refusing to take it from him. Caroline could see how distressed and angry she was at the captain's words—and at what had resulted. It was obvious that she wanted the entire ugly scene to be forgotten as soon as possible.

For her part, Caroline was more than a little angry with the captain for having presumed on her and Mary Beth in such a fashion. She had not elected him to be the guardian of her morality. In fact, as the captain settled back in his seat, Caroline had a devilish impulse to request the flask from Taggart and lift it to her own mouth.

Mary Beth stirred and opened her eyes to look fearfully at Caroline. It was obvious that Mary Beth had been awake all this while and had heard everything. Caroline understood her fear. The violence that only a moment before had exploded to life within the narrow confines of this coach still hung in the air, an almost palpable curtain between Dirk Taggart and the captain.

Was that a hint of laughter she caught in the Apache's brooding eyes? Caroline wondered. Or was it contempt for the fine pretensions of white men, and especially for those of his captor? Caroline could not tell for sure, and with a weary shrug she turned her head to look out once more through the side window of the stagecoach.

They were entering a badlands, she noted. Truncated peaks and great boulders lay strewn over the landscape like the abandoned playing blocks of some titanic child. The coach rocked violently as they turned into a canyon. She heard the driver crack his whip and cry out to his horses. A moment later, the shadow of a great wall of rock fell over them.

And at once it was cooler.

Perched high above the backs of the galloping horses, in the driver's seat beside Tim Moody, Seth reached down and grabbed his shotgun, then glanced over at Tim. The stage driver had said nothing to him, of course, but Seth knew enough to realize that if any attempt was going to be made on this gold shipment, this canyon would be the ideal place.

Tim Moody had caught Seth's motion. "Just make sure she's loaded and the safety is off," he said quietly, without even glancing in Seth's direction.

Seth nodded, smiling to himself. Moody, as usual, was way ahead of him. After checking out the shotgun as suggested, he rested the heavy weapon across his knees and kept his gaze on the trail ahead, alert for trouble.

Seth was almost twenty years old. For three years, he had ridden shotgun for Tim Moody on this Fort Laramie-to-Cheyenne run, in the hope that someday he would become a Jehu himself. Indeed, over the years Tim had labored mightily to teach Seth all he knew about driving a stage, which was a considerable amount. But on this particular trip—contrary to what had become usual practice—Moody had not let him take the reins once.

And Seth knew why. Tim Moody was disappointed in him. It was not something Seth had done. Rather, it was something he was planning to do—once they arrived in Cheyenne. Perhaps he should not have told Tim his plans, but Seth looked upon the Jehu almost as a father. Not to share with Moody what was on his mind—his hopes, his dreams—was impossible.

And so he had told Tim that he no longer planned to

become a stage driver for Wells Fargo, but an engineer with the Union Pacific instead.

Seth had wrestled with the decision for months, torn between his loyalty to the Jehu and Wells Fargo and his fascination with the steam locomotive. On every trip to Cheyenne since the railhead and the roundhouse had been established there in November 1867, he had made it his business to be on hand when a steam engine pulled in. To see those snorting, clanging iron horses hurtling along those gleaming steel tracks, to feel the thunder of their approach, to watch the great plume of black smoke—its underbelly livid with flame—had been more than enough to convince Seth that nothing in the world could equal the thrill of thrusting home the throttle of such a magnificent steed.

If only that desire had not put a wall between him and Tim Moody. His eyes on the twisting road ahead, both his hands closed firmly around the shotgun, Seth heaved a troubled sigh.

Beside him, Moody heard the sigh and understood. But he said nothing to the young man, just kept chewing on the unlit cigar in his mouth. His disappointment and hurt feelings were now a thing of the past. These last few days, he'd had a chance to do some thinking, and he'd come to the conclusion that there wasn't any reason why a fellow like Seth shouldn't go ahead and do with his life what he wanted. If Seth hankered after driving one of them newfangled steam engines, then that was his business. And more power to him, by grannies.

Besides, Moody reminded himself, who was he to find fault with Seth's decision to leave Wells Fargo when he himself was giving serious thought to the widow Crouse's offer to help her run that boardinghouse of hers in Cheyenne? Of course, Moody knew what that offer of Sarah Crouse's implied. Marriage! It was the thought of that awesome entanglement that had caused him to hold off his decision for so long. But hell, Sarah Crouse set a fine table and wasn't such a chore to look at, either. No, she sure as hell wasn't.

Moody chomped down decisively on his cigar. Like Seth, he had just about made up his mind. Glancing at Seth, he smiled to himself and decided he would give the young man the reins as soon as they put this canyon behind them.

His eyes on the treacherous, winding road ahead of him, Moody handled the reins like the artist he was. The most important talent any Wells Fargo driver could have was a way with horses, an intuitive awareness of what the animals he controlled might do under almost any circumstances—that, and a commanding hand on the reins. A capable reinsman did not need to lash his horses or crack the whip ceaselessly to indicate what he wanted. Instead, he had the ability to talk to his horses through the ribbons, as Moody liked to put it.

Tim Moody held both pairs of reins wrapped in the fingers of his left hand, on which—so as not to lose any sensitivity—he wore a light buckskin glove. His right hand he kept free for the friction brake and the whip. Unlike less-skilled drivers, Moody had the ability to guide his team without harnessing them as a single unit. Instead, he allowed the two pairs of horses below him to operate independently while he controlled them through his ribbons, sending the leaders into a turn while holding the wheelers steady until just the right moment. This was not a simple feat, and sudden disaster could befall any driver who botched it—animals becoming tangled and falling, with the coach crashing into them, perhaps even overturning.

It was a skill Tim had managed to teach Seth only

after months of patient effort. Now Seth was almost ready to handle a team himself. In fact, only a week earlier he had reminded his superiors that in young Seth Loman they already had a driver capable of taking over this run to Cheyenne.

Only, Seth was no longer interested, Tim reminded himself ruefully. Too bad. He would have made one fine Jehu—something this stage line would need for years to come. Those damn steam locomotives couldn't go everywhere—and where they couldn't go, the stagecoach would be going, and for some time to come. . . .

Abruptly, all consideration of the future of the stage line vanished from Moody's thoughts as the coach swept around a bend and he saw what was waiting for them.

"My God, Tim!" Seth cried. "Look at that!"

"I seen it, Seth!" Moody replied, snatching up his whip.

What both men saw looming ahead of them was a huge boulder resting squarely in the middle of the road—a barrier calculated to bring the stage to a scrambling halt.

"Keep that shotgun ready!" Moody cried.

"Ain't you gonna slow down?" Seth cried, peering anxiously around for the highwaymen who had rolled that formidable obstacle into their path.

"Hell no, I ain't stopping!"

Cracking his whip over the backs of his horses, Moody yanked the reins, sending the lead team suddenly to the right, directly at a short, steep embankment. The highwaymen who had dumped that boulder in the path of the stage didn't know this canyon as well as Moody did. The horses reached the low bank and scrambled up it onto the shelf beyond. A second later, lurching dangerously to the left, the stage struck the embankment. For a moment

Moody thought he had finally found an obstacle too formidable even for this Concord coach as it rocked precariously on its thoroughbraces. But the wheels and the undercarriage held. The coach straightened up and rumbled after the plunging horses—straight at a canyon wall.

Sweeping past a tall finger of rock, the stage veered away from the rock wall, and kept on toward a boulder-strewn stretch of ground, beyond which lay a narrow trail that led between the sheer rock wall and the boulder. Skillfully, deftly, Moody directed the team around the boulders toward the trail. The huge boulder reappeared on their left, the rock wall on their right. The space between these two massive obstacles, and through which the stagecoach would have to navigate, was narrow—perhaps too narrow.

Moody flung away his cigar. "Hang on!" he cried to Seth. "This is going to be a close one!"

The horses plunged past the boulder and into the narrow gap. Moody felt Seth leaning toward him as the coach rocked in after them. There was a grinding, unpleasant scraping sound that lasted for a second or two—and then the stagecoach was past the boulder, rattling along the ledge on the other side.

The low embankment loomed just ahead of them, with the road just beyond. Without hesitation, Moody swung his horses toward it. They scrambled down the short embankment. Standing up, Moody snaked his whip over their backs and reined them sharply to the right. Galloping wildly now, foam flecking their bits, the horses yanked the stage after them down the steep bank. As the coach crunched down onto the road, it tipped far over, barely remaining upright as it slewed violently to the right and careened after the horses.

Above the fierce clatter of the stage, Moody did not

hear the shot. But he felt the bullet that struck him—a searing thunderbolt of lead that caught him high in the back, just below his left shoulder. He sat down heavily in his seat, somehow managing to keep his grip on the reins. A darkness was falling over his eyes, and he felt himself sagging precariously to the left, away from Seth—and then his right foot was slipping awkwardly into space. Dimly, he heard another shot—more of an echo than the shot itself—and tried to warn Seth.

"Watch out, Seth!" he managed. "Them bastards are shootin' at us!"

Seth did not have to be told. Dropping his shotgun down into the boot, he pulled Moody back onto his seat, then snatched the reins from his hand and slapped them smartly down upon the horses' backs.

"Hi, yah!" he cried. *"Yah! Yah!"*

The four horses responded magnificently, surging forward with lengthening strides. It was almost as if they knew of Moody's wound and were as dismayed and as anxious as Seth was to get out of the highwaymen's range. The sound of the stage's powerful wheels rolling over the hard ground, together with the pounding of the horses' hooves, filled the canyon with an almost deafening roar.

From below him, Seth heard the faint cries of his outraged passengers as they were flung helplessly around inside the coach. But Seth could spare no time for explanations. He glanced over at Moody. The man had managed to slump down over the seat, his knees on the footboard, both hands hugging the back of the seat. In that single glance, Seth saw the dark patch of blood growing on the back of Tim's shoulder. Seth swore angrily and reached down and grabbed the whip, anxious to move still faster.

That was when Seth was hit, as well.

At almost the same time that he heard the faint crack

of a rifle shot from the canyon wall above him, he felt the slug slam into his thigh. The force of the round was such that it almost pushed him off the seat. He dropped the whip and saw it vanish beneath the wheels. Boosting himself back into the seat, he was able to hang on to the reins somehow and keep the horses moving, occasionally managing a wild but shaky cry to goad them on still faster.

At last the stage swept out from the confines of the canyon. Glancing back, Seth thought he saw two dim figures on one of the rims of the canyon, sunlight glinting on their rifles. He turned back around and urged his horses to still-greater speed. It would be only a matter of time, he realized, before those frustrated highwaymen mounted up and galloped after them.

But a few miles farther, when there appeared not to be any pursuit from the highwaymen, Seth allowed the weary, lathered horses to pull up. The moment the stage ground to a halt, a terrible, leaden fogginess fell over him, and he found he could barely manage the task of climbing down from the driver's seat.

By that time the doors of the coach had been flung open and the irate passengers were piling out of the stage. Seth found himself confronted by the captain, who looked as if his face had struck against something hard and unyielding.

"Just what in hell was the cause of that, mister?" he cried.

"Now hold off on the boy," warned the thin, pale fellow whom Seth took for a gambler. His voice was cold, but he appeared to be looking at Seth with some compassion—though he, too, seemed to have been knocked around during that wild, lurching flight through the canyon.

With a slight smile on his death's-head of a face, he

asked, "What happened, kid? What was *that* all about? Indians?"

It was difficult for Seth to believe, but none of the passengers had heard the shots that had struck not only their driver but their express messenger as well.

"Highwaymen," Seth explained, aware that his voice was high and thin, close to hysteria. It was his wound, he realized. His right leg from the thigh down was as heavy as a tie rail, and unnaturally warm from the strong flow of fresh blood.

"Highwaymen?" one of the women cried, aghast.

"My God! Look at his thigh!" said the other woman, her voice warm with sudden compassion. "He's been shot!"

"The driver, too," Seth said weakly. "Someone help me get him down. He's hurt bad, I think."

There was no need for Seth to explain any more. The captain and the gambler managed to lift Tim Moody down from his seat and place him inside the coach on the middle bench. As soon as Moody stretched out, one of the women—the one who was wearing the red dress—pressed the snout of a whiskey flask into his mouth, and Seth saw with some relief the gusto with which Moody gulped down the fiery liquid.

"You goin' to be all right, Tim?" Seth asked anxiously as he leaned over the wounded driver.

"It feels like someone stuck a hot branding iron down my back, Seth. But I hurt so bad, I know I'm gonna live. Go on back up there now and get us the hell out of here. Them bastards'll soon be after that gold. They ain't finished with us yet."

Seth pulled away and stepped down out of the stagecoach. As he turned to climb back up into the driver's seat, he heard someone coming after him. He turned. It was the woman who had ridden with the coach all the way from Billings. He remembered her name was Caroline Wells.

"What about you?" she asked, her voice filled with concern as it had been when she first saw his bloodstained Levi's.

"I'm all right," Seth said weakly, aware that his mouth was as dry as sandpaper. "It only nicked me. It's just bleedin' some, is all."

"You sure of that?" the captain asked, coming up behind Caroline and peering at him closely. "You don't look so good."

"Well, somebody's got to drive this stage, and I'm good enough for that. But I'd like one of you men to ride shotgun. We ain't out of the woods yet. Like Tim just said, them highwaymen could be on our trail right now. They must have seen Tim get hit, so they know we're hurtin'."

"I'd like to help," said the captain, "but I've got to stay down in the coach with my prisoner. I don't trust him the length of a gun barrel."

The gambler pulled up alongside the captain. He had heard Seth's request. "Sorry, kid," he said, shaking his head ruefully. "I'm in no shape to sit up there beside you. I'd only fall off and add to your troubles." He smiled thinly. "I just ain't got the strength. And this whiskey I been pullin' on ain't about to give it to me, either." Then the gambler turned to the captain. "If you ride shotgun, I'll keep an eye on the Apache for you."

"Not on your life, mister. I'd trust you less than the Apache."

"Well, I can't stand here and argue," said Seth wearily. He turned and started to climb up into the driver's seat.

"I'll ride shotgun!"

Seth turned. Yes, he had heard correctly. It was Caroline Wells who was offering. He almost laughed until he saw the serious, determined look on her face.

"Now, ma'am," he said, "that's right brave of you, but I think you'd better ride in the coach and keep an eye on Tim Moody."

"Mary Beth and I'll keep an eye on Mr. Moody, young man," said the woman in the red dress. "You get up there and drive—and let this young woman ride shotgun. I got a hunch she'll do as good as any man."

"Besides," Caroline said quickly, "we can't stand here forever and argue about it."

With a weary shrug, Seth gave in and hauled himself up onto the driver's seat. A moment later a flushed, excited Caroline Wells climbed up beside him.

Brushing a lock of hair out of her eyes, she said, almost breathlessly, "Where's the shotgun?"

"In the boot, miss."

"You can call me Caroline," she said, grabbing hold of the barrel of the shotgun and hauling it up beside her.

"Sure, ma'am," Seth said. "Just keep your eye on the trail behind us and let me know when you see any riders comin' after us. And try to keep them double barrels down. The piece is fully loaded and the safety catch is off."

"I'll be careful with it," the young woman said. "Don't you worry none. My dad taught me how to shoot as soon as I could ride."

"That's just fine," Seth managed, aware of a cold sweat standing out on his forehead.

Without another word, he gathered up the reins and gave the horses as brisk a slap as he could under the circumstances. They started up, slowly at first. But under repeated urgings from Seth, they leaned into their harnesses, lifted their legs under them, and began to gallop once more. Spent though they were, they still had enough iron in their legs—and in their hearts—to give it another grand effort. Soon, the stagecoach was rolling swiftly over the road on its way to Devil's Creek, the next way station.

The horses would make it, Seth realized. The question was: *Would he?*

Hanging on to the rocking coach as best she could, Caroline stole a glance at the young driver. She could not help but note his pale face, the sweat beading his forehead, and the spreading bloodstain on his Levi's. That wound of his was continuing to bleed, and she wondered if she shouldn't be doing something about it.

She cleared her throat. "What's your name, driver?"

"Seth, ma'am," he said, quickly glancing over his shoulder at the road behind him.

"Seth, I think you're likely losing a lot of blood— maybe too much if you're going to drive."

Seth nodded miserably and glanced at Caroline. "Guess maybe you're right, ma'am. I can feel the blood in my boot. But we ain't got the time to see to it. And I wish you'd keep an eye out behind us while I drive this team."

Without replying, Caroline reached under her dress and tore away the bottom of her slip. It made a snarling sound as it ripped, and Seth glanced over at her in surprise. But Caroline paid no attention. This was no time for niceties. Balling up the heavy strip of cotton, she handed it to Seth.

"Here," she told him. "Use this to stop the bleeding. When you get it over the wound, I'll get another piece to wind around your thigh. Go ahead now. I'll take the reins."

"You can't do that, ma'am," Seth protested. "You

can't handle these reins. The horses will get away from you."

"Just for a minute—while you reach down into your pants and do as I say. Do you want me to do it for you while you drive?"

"Oh no, ma'am," Seth said quickly, handing the reins to Caroline.

Caroline kept the reins for only a few seconds and did not look as Seth loosened his Levi's and positioned the heavy wad of cotton over his wound. Swiftly, he buttoned himself back up and took the reins from Caroline.

Despite the gravity of the situation, Caroline had some difficulty keeping the smile off her face as she saw how scarlet Seth's cheeks were. But he needn't have worried—she had kept her eyes on the road ahead. Bending once again, she tore off a longer strip from the bottom of her cotton slip and, before the young man could protest, proceeded to wrap it tightly around his thigh. She finished by tying the bandage with a square knot, then took up the double-barreled shotgun once again and looked back at the trail behind them, searching for signs of danger. But there were none. The road coiling through the pine-studded landscape was clear of riders. The canyon itself was now little more than a dim cap on the blistering horizon.

She turned back around and glanced at Seth. He seemed a little better—his hands were no longer trembling. She took a deep breath. She had never felt this excited before, or so pleased with herself. So this was how it was to experience real danger. It should have horrified her. Instead, it filled her with a sense of being alive—fully and completely alive.

She watched the landscape flowing by. It did not seem so desolate, so threatening, from up here beside the driver. Yes, that was it. She was out of that stagecoach, no longer cooped up with that somber Indian and that oh-so-correct cavalry officer—or that dying man, the consumptive whose only solace seemed to be his whiskey flask. Now she had something to take her mind off her brother—and her father waiting back in Montana Territory. Now, at last, she had something to do.

Chapter 3

Kyle Warner was cursing himself with deadly intensity. Teaming up with this crew of cutthroats had been a fool idea to begin with, and now he was reaping the harvest his folly had sown.

When the stagecoach had gone through the canyon and he had seen Will and Luke opening up on the driver, Kyle had drawn on both men in an effort to prevent bloodshed. The result had been a sudden, deadly gunfight between the three brothers and Kyle. At first Kyle had the element of surprise on his side, but that advantage was long gone now. At the moment, he was crouching down behind a shoulder-high boulder, quickly reloading his smoking gun, hoping to get another clear shot at Luke Donner. But Luke was already out of sight in the rocks behind him, and Kyle wasn't sure where Will and Flem were at that moment. He had last seen them ducking back into the shadows of the canyon below.

He caught another glimpse of Luke clambering up the steep slope and snapped off a quick shot. He saw a tiny explosion on the sheet of rock just above Luke where the round struck, and he knew he had missed. Luke vanished from sight. From the look of it, Luke would soon be high enough to direct a deadly fusillade down on Kyle.

The only thing left for him was get to the horses—and fast.

Turning and crouching low, Kyle swiftly descended the steep slope. Though he had succeeded in preventing the three brothers from riding after the stage, it bothered him that he had been unable to keep them from firing on it as it swept beneath them and out of the canyon. Kyle had been thunderstruck when the Jehu drove his team up onto that low shelf and then rammed the stagecoach through that opening between the boulder and the rock. The four of them had labored mightily to dislodge that boulder and send it crashing down onto the road—all to no avail.

Kyle jumped lightly to the floor of the canyon and cautiously looked around. Will and Flem were around here somewhere, but when he had seen them last they had been hightailing it deeper into the canyon.

Keeping to the shadows, his gun at the ready, Kyle moved swiftly along the base of the rock wall that now towered over him. He was grateful for its protection, but he knew it wouldn't be long before one of the three spotted him and figured where he was going.

He realized now the folly of having thought he could so easily control the lawlessness of these three brothers. When he had overheard them making their plans in Fort Laramie, he had immediately concluded that he would have no trouble at all handling such ignorant, worthless types. Indeed, it had seemed to him that he had stumbled upon the perfect setup. The holdup of the stage would have created an ideal smoke screen for his rescue of Santoro and for the Apache chieftain's subsequent disappearance.

Kyle had been certain that after the holdup it would have been a simple matter for him to disarm his three confederates, take the gold, and return it to the Wells

Fargo people as soon as the opportunity afforded itself. He had never been able to make this part of his scheme entirely clear in his mind, but the point was that he had no intention of keeping the gold or profiting in any way from the holdup. He also had no intention of turning the three brothers in. He would have been content simply to disarm them, truss them up, and leave them behind while he and Santoro rode off.

As Kyle went over all this in his mind once again, he saw more clearly than ever how chancy his plan had been from the very beginning. In his eagerness to free Santoro, he had allowed his enthusiasm for this scheme to override his good sense. Shaking his head ruefully at his temerity, Kyle carefully slipped around a finger of rock, then into the narrow passageway that led to the grassy sward where they had tethered their horses.

He breathed a sigh of relief when he saw all four horses still there, patiently cropping the grass at their feet.

Moving swiftly, he holstered his Colt and untied the horses from the saplings rimming the small meadow. He was preparing to mount his own horse when Will Donner stepped out into the small clearing, his revolver in his hand.

His voice cold with measured fury, Will said, "We figured this is where you'd head, you double-crossing sonofabitch."

Behind Will came Flem. He too carried a six-gun and, like Will, had it trained on Kyle's gut. As Flem stepped out in full view and took his place beside his brother, he rubbed one hand over the wiry stubble that covered his face, and with his small, mean eyes regarded Kyle almost hungrily. There was no doubt in Kyle's mind what Will and Flem intended to do now that they had cornered him.

"Get out away from them horses, mister," Will said, "so we can see what a damn sonofabitch like you looks like before he takes it in the gut."

But Kyle had other ideas.

Vaulting into his saddle and drawing his weapon—all in one swift motion—he fired on Will, then clapped spurs to his mount. The round caught the outlaw squarely in his chest, stamping a neat black hole in his shirt. Will buckled but did not go down. A curse on his lips, the outlaw managed to get off a shot at Kyle, but it went wild. Glancing back at Will, Kyle snapped a second shot at him, then fired over the other horses' heads, catapulting them into an instant stampede. As Kyle spurred his mount after the fleeing horses, a shot from behind seared the air over his right shoulder. He glanced back to see Flem steadying his aim for a second shot. Kyle flung a round at Flem, turned around in his saddle, and—keeping his head low— galloped after the stampeding horses.

Flem managed to send two more rounds after him, but each one found nothing solid, and a moment later Kyle swept around a massive boulder and out of Flem's line of sight. He kept after the stampeding horses, driving them ahead of him, and in a few minutes he had left the canyon. As he rode on out of it, a single, almost despairing rifle shot echoed in the air behind him. Kyle turned in his saddle to see the third brother, Luke, standing on a high rim, slowly lowering his rifle.

Kyle turned back around. Ahead of him, the stampeding horses were slowing down and beginning to disperse. He decided against keeping them going with another shot and concentrated on the road ahead. He had a stagecoach to catch.

*   *   *

"How is he?" Luke asked Flem, leaning his rifle against the rock face and kneeling beside his brother Will.

"That sonofabitch got him twice," Flem said, shaking his head bitterly. "Once in the chest and the second time in the side. He ain't dead yet, Luke, but he's a wishin' he were."

Luke lifted Will's hands from his chest and cursed softly. Will's fingers were slick with his own blood, and the open chest cavity bubbled with escaping air from each labored breath the dying man took. Luke let Will's hands rest back down over the wound and peered into his brother's face.

"Will?" he asked. "Can you hear me?"

Will's lidded eyes flicked open. The man appeared to be angry with Luke. "What you want? I'm dyin'—let me be."

"I know that, Will," Luke said fiercely, "but I want you to know we'll find that sonofabitch and get him for you. We'll kill him. Slow like. That's a promise."

"Hell, I knowed that. Now let me be, will you? This here hurts like hell—I can feel the blood filling up my chest . . . like I'm fit to burst. Now just let me be."

"Sure, Will," Luke said, standing up.

Will closed his eyes again. He seemed to settle into the ground somewhat, but the brothers could see his still-heaving chest and knew he remained alive.

Then Will began to cough. A thin ribbon of blood trickled from one corner of his mouth. He stopped coughing and opened his eyes, searching for his brothers. His two big hands still cradling his leaking chest, he muttered, "Adios, you two."

"Yeah, good-bye, Will," said Flem. Luke just nodded.

Will closed his eyes. His head rolled loosely to one

side, and his hands fell away from his chest. A final shudder, then the lungs were still.

A single tear rolled down Luke's grimy face as he turned to Flem. "I'll bury him. You start after them horses."

Flem nodded soberly, turned, and, with one last backward glance, started down the canyon. As he ran, he thought of only one thing—what he would do to that double-crossing sonofabitch when he caught up to him.

And they *would* catch up to him. Of that Flem had no doubt at all.

It was late in the day, and Seth had let the horses come to a complete halt. A steep grade lifted before them, and the horses needed the chance to blow some. Seth called down to his passengers to let them know why he had halted, and for a moment all Caroline could hear was the snorting of the lead horse and the faint jingle of the harness. The silence was awesome.

Then she heard something odd. It disturbed her, but she couldn't be sure what it was. She heard it again just as Seth snapped his reins over the backs of the horses. At once the four beasts leaned into their harnesses, hooves digging, and the stage lurched forward, heading for the ridge.

That was when Caroline realized what she had heard.

She grabbed Seth's hand. "Hold it, Seth!" she cried. "Stop the stage! I think I heard gunfire! It's coming from the other side of that ridge!"

Seth looked at her. It was obvious that he had heard nothing, but by this time he was too weak to argue with the woman. Closing his eyes wearily, he hauled back on the reins, then applied the brake to bring the stage to a scrambling halt.

"What's wrong?" cried Captain Farnum from below. "Why are we stopping again?"

"Caroline thinks she heard something," Seth called out as he slowly, painfully, descended to the ground. Caroline—still holding on to the shotgun—climbed down after him.

The door of the stage opened and Farnum, followed by the gambler, Taggart, stepped out. "You say you heard something?" the captain asked Caroline, somewhat impatiently.

"Yes," snapped Caroline. "Gunfire. And if you'll listen a moment, you might hear it, too."

So for a moment they stood there, listening. Caroline began to feel silly—until suddenly all of them heard the sound of high, yipping voices, followed by a weak fusillade of shots.

"That's gunfire, sure enough!" said Farnum. "And it sounds like Indians."

"It's the way station at Devil's Creek," said Seth. "The Sioux are after the horses."

"Stay here and take care of that Apache of yours," Taggart told the captain. "Seth and I'll go up onto that ridge and take a look-see."

"I'm going, too," Caroline told them.

With a shrug, Taggart said, "Come along, then. But keep your head down."

The three of them hurried up the road, but it was Caroline who led the way. Seth was having difficulty because of his wound, and Taggart broke into a cold sweat the moment he began to run. Nevertheless, the two men stayed close behind Caroline, exhibiting a dogged courage that impressed her.

As soon as they reached the crest of the ridge, they ducked into the rocks beside the road and peered down at the broad valley floor below them. Devil's Creek wound in a lazy meander through the valley, and just below them, tucked cozily into one of its broad bends, were the log house and barns of the way station.

It was around those three buildings that a war party of mounted Sioux were galloping. The sporadic firing from the log house seemed to be keeping the Sioux at a distance, but for how long, Caroline dared not guess. Even as Caroline watched, she saw three Sioux break off from the attack on the log house and head for the barns and corrals.

Seth turned to Caroline. "Go back and get the captain," he told her. "You can watch that Apache for him. Hurry. Ty Wilks and his wife can't hold out much longer. Sounds to me like they're already low on ammunition."

Caroline wanted to stay with the men, but she saw the wisdom in Seth's suggestion and went back for the captain. He listened to what she told him, then thrust his revolver into her hand, took the shotgun she was carrying, and hurried toward the crest.

Caroline ducked her head into the stage. She saw the two women huddled inside, staring with numb terror at the Apache, who was still looking straight ahead, apparently without a single thought concerning these two terrified females sitting across from him. Tim Moody was conscious, and turned his head to look at Caroline. The whiskey flask was resting on his chest, his gloved hand closed around it.

Waggling the revolver at the Indian, she said to him, "All right, get out, Mister Apache. You and I are going over to those rocks where it's cool." Then she stepped back.

Without any indication that he had heard her, the Apache, moving with great dignity and as silently as a shadow, leaned forward and stepped out of the stage. As he came to a halt in front of Caroline, she thought she detected a tiny flicker of amusement in his dark, liquid eyes.

Clearing her throat nervously, Caroline called into the stage, "Why don't the rest of you come out here, too? I think it would be good for Tim. It's much cooler in the rocks."

A rustle of skirts presaged the two women's appearance in the doorway. Mary Beth looked with some wonder at the revolver in Caroline's hands, while there was a slight smile on Louise Thompson's face as she stepped down.

"You handle that hogleg with real ease," she told Caroline. "Looks like we don't have nothing to worry about—from this here Apache, anyway."

Then the two women reached back into the stage and helped the driver out of it. Leaning heavily on both women, Moody managed a weak grin.

"Looks like I'm getting some right nice attention from you gals," he said. "Lead the way."

Caroline turned to Santoro and directed him to move ahead of them toward the rocks. As she followed after the Indian, she could hear faintly the sound of gunfire coming from the valley beyond the ridge. She shuddered involuntarily. Seth had said that he didn't think the man and wife in the way station had much ammunition left. And that meant it could all be over in a matter of minutes, she realized, with only those three men—one of them a pale consumptive, another weak from loss of blood—between them and the Sioux.

There had been no argument from Taggart or Seth when Farnum told each man curtly and without apology that he would direct what he chose to call the reconnaissance. And as Farnum led his two recruits down through the rocks to Devil's Creek, he found himself pleased to be once again in action against the American "aborigines" —as his instructor at West Point, Colonel Pelton, had insisted on calling them.

Undetected by the Sioux war party, Farnum reached the creek and plunged into the waist-high water, Taggart and Seth following in after him. The creek, fed by mountain snow, was ice cold and very swift. For a moment Farnum thought Taggart was going to be swept away. He reached out to steady him, then pulled him in close to the bank. Seth was already hugging the bank, and it was clear to Farnum that the man was not at his best. Farnum couldn't be positive, but he thought the water around Seth's waist was darkening with blood from his wound.

Well, it didn't matter now, Farnum realized grimly. They had to get closer to that cabin, surprise the Sioux from the rear, and bring down as many as they could in their first salvo. The war party had no idea that another force was in the vicinity, and it was this element of surprise that Farnum was counting on to rout the Indians and relieve the way station's defenders.

Pushing on through the icy water and keeping as close to the bank as they could, they finally reached a heavy stand of willows within 150 yards of the cabin. Crouching in the brush on the edge of the willows, the three men were afforded a clear, unobstructed view of the cabin and of the Sioux war party.

There were five Sioux—firing as they rode—still circling the station house. Farnum glimpsed five more in the fields some distance away, rounding up the station's horses. Closer, two Sioux were leading a couple of fine horses from one of the barns, and even as Farnum glanced in their direction, he saw the nearest barn begin to burn. As the flames leaped out one window, a shrieking Sioux raced from the barn, a blazing brand held triumphantly over his head.

Emboldened by this, the Sioux circling the station house dismounted and, *ki-yiing,* raced toward it. A single shot from within caught one of the Sioux and sent him spinning to the ground. The other four paused momentarily to look back at their fallen comrade, then continued on to the station house. There were no further shots from within, and Farnum realized why. The defenders were out of ammunition.

The Indians disappeared inside the building. Farnum heard a woman scream. Unable to hold himself back any longer, he jumped up from the willows and dashed across the ground toward the station house without glancing back once to see if the other two were following. A Sioux brandishing a war lance raced from one of the barns to intercept him. Farnum waited until the Indian was close enough, then blew him away with a blast from one barrel of his shotgun.

Another Sioux, in front of the burning barn, went down on one knee and brought his rifle up to his shoulder. Before he finished tracking Farnum, a gunshot from just behind Farnum brought the Indian down. Farnum glanced back to see who had fired—it was the gambler, Taggart. The man was panting, his bone-white face revealing the awful effort it took for him to keep up with Farnum. Seth was nowhere in sight.

Farnum looked back at the station house and found that he was only a few yards away from it.

Out through the doorway bolted two Indians. With his remaining barrel, Farnum cut the first in half. As the next Sioux came at him, Farnum swung the shotgun like a club, catching the Indian on the side of the head. But the man was seemingly indestructible, and flung himself on Farnum. As Farnum went down under the furious charge, he heard another shot just behind him. The Indian peeled away from Farnum, clutching at his head as he did so. Farnum scrambled to his feet.

"Here, Captain," cried Taggart. "Seth's too far gone to use it."

Farnum turned just in time to catch the six-gun Taggart threw at him. Spinning, he found himself confronting a third Sioux, who was plunging out of the station building. The Indian flung up his rifle and was preparing to fire. Farnum struck the rifle barrel aside, then clubbed the Sioux to the ground with the barrel of Seth's revolver.

Farnum raced into the building, Taggart right behind him. The fourth Sioux, an ax buried in his skull, was on the floor beside the fallen stationmaster. As Taggart hurried to the side of the stationmaster's wife, huddled in a corner of the kitchen, Farnum found a window and looked out. The rest of the Sioux, astride their ponies, were stampeding the station's horseflesh ahead of them as they swiftly rode away. They had had enough, it appeared.

They had stolen the horses, but, thanks to Farnum and Taggart, they had paid a stiff price.

Caroline had given Louise Thompson the captain's huge revolver and asked her to guard the Apache while she hurried to the crest of the road to see what was happening in the valley below.

She had seen the Sioux rush the station and had watched breathlessly as the captain and Taggart charged out of the willows after them. The running gun battle with the Sioux had left her numb, but when she saw the rest of the Sioux riding off with the stolen horses, she breathed a sigh of relief—and shook her head in wonder that two men who had acted with such hatred toward each other in the stagecoach could have banded together for such a courageous act. She was convinced that she would always remember that charge to the stationmaster's house as the most gallant action she had ever witnessed. She no longer felt so superior to Captain Farnum. He might seem at first glance to be only spit and polish, but there was obviously much more to the man than that.

Now, as Caroline saw Farnum trudging up the road toward her, she ran to meet him. He pulled up wearily in front of her and asked if she could drive the stagecoach down to the station house. Not long after, with Caroline handling the reins, the stage and its passengers pulled up in front of the way station.

Caroline had been warned by Farnum to expect a rather bloody sight when she drove into the yard. But as she clambered down from the driver's seat—cursing modestly at her long skirts—she saw no dead Indians littering the yard. Then she saw the gambler approaching the stage from the direction of a barn that was now little more than a smoldering shell. He looked like death incarnate as he trudged wearily toward them. His dark suit and shirt were stained with blood, and his pale face had a gaunt, terrible look about it.

Then she realized what he must have been doing at the still-burning barn, and where those dead Indians were. She shuddered.

Taggart came to a halt in front of Caroline. "That lady inside is in quite a state," he told her. "I hope you women can calm her down some. Her husband's been hurt pretty bad, looks like."

Caroline nodded. "Mary Beth and I will go right in," she told the man.

But it took a while for them to get the injured Moody into the station house, where he was put down on a cot beside the stationmaster, who already had a makeshift bandage wrapped around his head. His wife, trembling and weeping, was hovering over him. And, as Taggart had warned them, she seemed entirely too distracted to be of much assistance. Indeed, it was her husband who appeared to be the one offering comfort.

And Caroline knew why. Farnum had already told her what had happened when the Sioux broke into the station. A Sioux brave had struck down the stationmaster and was busy scalping him when his wife buried a meat ax in the Indian's head. No wonder she was still hysterical; as far as Caroline was concerned, she had a perfect right to be.

Louise Thompson and Mary Beth gently drew the woman away from her husband. She turned, took one look at Mary Beth, and buried her face in her shoulder. As Mary Beth comforted her, Louise hurried over to the sink for a cup of water.

Caroline frowned. Someone was missing. And then she remembered—Seth Loman. As Captain Farnum started past her on his way out of the building, she reached out and took his arm. "Captain, where's Seth?"

"I don't know. Taggart left him in a clump of willows when we charged the station house. But when he went back after him, he was gone. Seth must have crawled off when the Sioux got too close. He had lost some blood, and there's a good chance he's out of his head."

"Then someone should go after him."

"I agree, ma'am," the captain replied courteously. "And Dirk Taggart and I will be going after him soon as we finish forting this place up in case those Sioux decide to come back—the Sioux or those highwaymen who tried to rob us back there."

"I'm going after him now, before it gets dark."

"I wouldn't advise that, ma'am. There might be some Sioux out there yet. We punished them pretty bad, and they might be thinking of coming back and making us pay a little more for what we did to them."

"All the more reason for me to go after Seth," she said, swiftly moving past the captain and out the door.

She was halfway across the yard when she heard someone call her name. She stopped and turned to see Louise Thompson hurrying after her. Smiling, Louise pulled up in front of Caroline and handed her the captain's enormous revolver, the one Caroline had given her earlier to guard the Apache.

Caroline took the hefty weapon and thanked Louise.

"I heard what you told that captain," Louise said. "I want to go with you. That kid could be hurt bad. A night under the stars wouldn't be good for him, not if he's lost much blood."

"Thank you, Louise. The captain said they left him in the willows. We'll try there first."

It was Louise who stumbled onto the wounded man's trail. Seth had gone a considerable distance on foot, evidently, before collapsing face down on the far side of the creek. From there, he had dragged himself through the grass like an enormous snake, leaving behind a slick trail of blood. It soon became obvious where he was heading— a rocky wasteland that overlooked the station.

Holding their skirts high, both women clambered up into the rocks. It was not long before they found Seth. He was sitting with his back propped up against a rock, his eyes closed. For a moment, as Caroline bent over him, it appeared to her that Seth was no longer breathing.

Then he opened his eyes and gazed up at her. He smiled faintly. "Hi, Miss Caroline."

"Hi, Seth. How do you feel?"

"Real funny," he told her. "Like I'm on a high lonesome, only I ain't had a drink in days."

Louise reached down and placed her hand on his forehead. She pulled it away and looked with alarm at Caroline. "He has a terrible fever," she said.

"Then we'd better get him back to the station," Caroline said. "You take his feet, and I'll carry him by the shoulders."

Before Caroline could reach down to grab Seth by the shoulder, a shadow fell over her. She turned to see a Sioux warrior, his war club held high over his head. His savage face was painted with hideous designs, and his eyes were cold and cruel. She didn't remember thinking about it, but the next thing she knew, the revolver Louise had given her was raised in her hand, exploding repeatedly as she kept squeezing the double-action trigger.

Without a single outcry, the Indian collapsed forward onto her, the weight of his dead body crushing her to the ground. Another Indian stepped out from behind the rocks. He had a rifle in his hand and pointed it down at Caroline. Unable to move, she found herself staring up at the bore of the rifle, waiting for the detonation. But it never came—for Louise flung herself at the Indian and knocked him backward. Almost casually the brave clubbed Louise aside, regained his balance, and brought his rifle up a second time. Caroline had never felt so helpless in her life. She wanted to cry out, but she knew it would be useless.

A rifle shot from above cracked sharply. The Indian, a startled look on his painted face, was driven forward by the force of the round. He hit the ground hard, then turned back around, bringing his rifle up to fire back at his assailant. But a second rifle shot from above drove the warrior into the ground, killing him instantly.

A moment later a tall fellow dressed in a buckskin

jacket and wearing a black plainsman's hat climbed down beside them. He introduced himself as Kyle Warner, and was in the act of helping a bloodied and considerably shaken Caroline to her feet when Taggart and Mary Beth, alerted by the gunfire, came running.

It was a sober party indeed that brought the now-unconscious Seth Loman back with them to the way station.

Chapter 4

Due to his own foolish complicity in that abortive stage holdup, Kyle felt considerably chastened as he approached the way station and witnessed at close hand the trials these passengers had endured this day. The stench of the burning barn hung heavily in the air around the buildings. He saw no bodies around, but he was almost certain he caught the dark, telltale stain of blood on a trampled portion of grass not too far from the station.

Kyle was carrying the unconscious express messenger in his arms. Beside him trudged the woman he had saved from the Sioux with the rifle. She had introduced herself as Caroline Wells, and he remembered her as one of the prettiest passengers to board the stage at Fort Laramie, but her rich, dark auburn curls were a sweaty tangle now, and her mint-green corduroy dress was bloodied and torn. Though he dared not look too closely, he could not help noticing that her underslip had been torn. Wisps of it trailed out from under her skirt as she walked. The other two women did not seem to be as disheveled as the Wells woman, but both of them looked bedraggled and close to hysteria.

Dirk Taggart was behind them, struggling to keep up with this sorry party. The day had obviously stretched his endurance to the breaking point. This Dirk Taggart was a far cry from the cool gambler Kyle had witnessed the night before. After making his deal with the Donners, Kyle had watched Taggart playing some pretty high-stakes poker in Fort Laramie's busiest gambling saloon. There, Taggart had looked as implacable as death, his lidded eyes and frozen countenance showing no emotion at all as he lost steadily to his raucous partners. But at last the cards began to turn in his favor, as they always did with a man of his skills. It was dawn when, coughing with almost feminine delicacy into his immaculate handkerchief, he excused himself, stood up, and, with a courtly bow to the frustrated players still in their chairs, swept his winnings off the table.

Kyle heard the man coughing. The sound was harsh, tearing. He paused momentarily and looked back at the gambler. "You going to be all right?"

"Never mind me," Taggart told him, his voice containing a surprising resonance and power. "It's that kid you're carrying we got to worry about."

Kyle continued on to the station house. Santoro's captor was standing in the doorway, waiting for them. The captain had obviously stayed behind to guard Santoro when the others had left to investigate the gunfire. Farnum's eyes were suspicious as they flicked over Kyle, but he said nothing as Kyle carried the express messenger past him and into the building.

The women hurried inside to help as Miranda Wilks, the wife of the stationmaster, brought out some winter blankets and an old straw mattress. The women swiftly fashioned a cot for Kyle's burden, and Kyle gently lowered the young man onto the mattress.

Straightening up, he looked around and saw two other cots nearer the wall, containing two other injured men. One of them—apparently the stationmaster—had a huge bloody bandage wrapped around his head. The other had his shirt off and his arm in a sling, with heavy bandages wound around his left shoulder. Kyle recognized this fellow as the driver of the stagecoach. At once Kyle found himself remembering the way the Donners had begun pouring fire down upon the stage as it swept past the boulder. Kyle had thought he had stopped the Donners' fire in time to prevent them from hitting anyone on the stage. Apparently, he had not been quick enough.

Santoro was standing in the corner, impassive, his wrists still shackled. Kyle did not dare let his gaze linger on the Apache for more than a second. But that second was enough. The moment the Apache's eyes met Kyle's, his face glowed with defiance—and hope.

"Who are you, mister?" Captain Farnum asked, pulling up in front of Kyle and making no effort to shake hands.

The captain was no fool, Kyle realized. It was obvious he suspected Kyle of being in cahoots with the highwaymen who had tried to rob the stage. At the same time, the captain—having glimpsed Kyle briefly in Fort Laramie—was attempting to recall where the two might have met before.

"Name's Kyle Warner," he said, extending his hand. "I own a ranch in Montana. I was on my way to Cheyenne to see about a beef contract with the railroad when I heard gunfire in the rocks. It was a good thing I did. That woman over there had finished off one of the savages, but another one was all set to finish her off."

"He saved my life, Captain," said Caroline Wells, hurrying over. "If it hadn't been for him, I'd . . . still be out there."

Reluctantly, the captain shook Kyle's hand. "How was it you happened by at this time?"

"I couldn't be sure, but I thought I heard gunfire earlier. If I hadn't, I might have ridden on past. I was planning on making my own camp tonight. No fire, of course—I've been hearing about the Sioux hereabouts."

Captain Farnum nodded grudgingly, his suspicions abating somewhat. "What you heard was right, Warner. Those two Sioux you saved Caroline from were left from a war party that was attacking this way station. Taggart and I managed to kill a few of them and disperse the rest. Where's your mount?"

"Tethered back there in the rocks. I'll be going after it in a minute."

"Good. If the Sioux haven't taken it, we have good use for it. The savages have managed to drive off all this station's fresh horses."

"Then I'd best go after my horse now," Kyle said, turning to leave the station building.

He was halfway out the door when Caroline Wells called his name. He paused in the doorway and turned as she hurried toward him. "I didn't thank you. I . . . I was too upset."

Kyle smiled and reached out to take her shoulder. "Why, that's all right, Miss Wells. I think you're a very brave woman. What you have just lived through would have turned any other woman I know into a hysterical wreck."

She nodded, smiling wanly. "It was awful," she said. "I still can't believe what I've done. It happened so . . . quick. And whenever I think that someone is dead because of me, I want to cry."

"It was you or that Indian, Miss Wells."

"But I feel so . . . unclean."

"If he had killed you, he would have been pleased—and proud. Don't forget that."

"I suppose so," she said uncertainly. "But that doesn't seem to help any."

"It probably never will," he told her soberly. "But it won't do any good to keep thinkin' on it. Best thing is to do what you can for those wounded men."

She nodded thoughtfully. "Yes," she said. "I suppose you're right."

"I sure do hope I am, Miss Wells."

He turned then and left her standing in the doorway. It was almost dusk, and he hoped Captain Farnum was off the mark when he suggested the Sioux might have taken his horse. It would also be nice, he told himself, if there were no more members of that war party lurking in the vicinity.

When Kyle returned to the way station with his horse—his scalp still intact—he found that Caroline Wells had done as he had suggested. Taking charge, she had encouraged Miranda Wilks to fashion a meal for all of them and had gotten the other two women passengers to clean up the large barn of a room, while she busied herself setting the long table.

The meal that followed was a tribute to the stationmaster's wife, and it was obvious to Kyle that the task of preparing it had done much to calm her down. It was not until later that night, while having a quiet smoke under the stars with Dirk Taggart, that he learned how effectively—and bloodily—the woman had come to her husband's aid earlier that same day.

The night was blessedly uneventful. Kyle and Taggart took turns standing guard outside the station house, while inside the captain slept alongside Santoro, his six-gun in his hand.

Morning dawned clear, and the stationmaster's wife

greeted it with a hearty, gut-filling breakfast for all of them. After checking on the condition of the wounded men, Kyle, Captain Farnum, and Taggart went outside to decide on their course of action. As they pulled up close to the burned-out barn, Kyle glanced back at the log building and saw that Santoro, his wrists still shackled, had been allowed to leave the station house and was now standing quietly beside the door, with Louise Thompson watching him. To his surprise, Kyle saw that the older woman was smoking a cheroot. This habit accounted for her somewhat gruff voice, he concluded.

Kyle had made no effort to help Santoro escape the night before. These passengers had been through enough already, and Kyle felt more than a little responsible for a good deal of their trouble. It was important that he not add anything to the load they already were carrying. So he had decided he would stay with them and not try to free Santoro until they reached Cheyenne. The passengers were going to need all the help they could get if they were to make it safely.

"Warner? You with us?"

Kyle quickly looked back at Farnum. "Sure, Captain. Go ahead. I'm listening."

"I was saying I'll have to remain inside the coach with my prisoner, and since Taggart here admits he's in no condition to drive the stage, I was wondering if you felt up to it."

"Me, drive the stage?"

"Do you have any other suggestion?"

Taggart said, "That Miss Wells could manage it, I'll bet."

"Never mind," said Kyle. "I have no doubt that she could. But I see no reason why I couldn't handle it."

"Good," said the captain. "Then I think it's time we

55

loaded up the stage. If you'll see to bringing out the horses, Taggart and I'll get the wounded ready. I'm worried about Ty Wilks. He won't die from that near-scalping, but him and his wife aren't going to be much help around here. Not for a while, anyway.''

"And those Sioux might come back," mused Kyle.

Taggart frowned. "Well, maybe I'd better stay behind," he said. "Give them two a hand looking after the station."

Farnum looked at the gambler with some surprise. "That's a pretty quick decision you just made. You sure you want to do it?"

"I'm sure."

"Done," said the captain.

There was no further discussion. The three men returned to the way station.

Tim Moody was the first to be helped into the stagecoach. Behind him came Seth Loman. Although Seth was exceedingly weak and was forced to lean on a makeshift crutch, he climbed into the stagecoach under his own power. The bullet was still lodged in Moody's shoulder and he was obviously in considerable pain, but the older man managed a smile as Seth eased himself into the seat facing him.

Louise Thompson, who had stayed by Seth's side as he walked out to the stage, was about to get in after him when she noticed Dirk Taggart standing by the station house door in his shirt sleeves, watching.

"Aren't you coming, Dirk?" she called.

Taggart shook his head. Louise hesitated, then left the coach and hurried over to the man. "Why are you staying?" she asked.

"To help the stationmaster look after things. Besides, I wasn't up to that ride into Cheyenne, anyway."

Louise looked back at the stage. Captain Farnum was approaching it with the Apache. She remembered the Apache's stony gaze, and the captain's erect formality.

"I don't think I'm up to it either," she said, looking back at Taggart. "Do you think Miranda would mind if I stayed behind to help her?"

For a moment Taggart's lidded eyes regarded her coldly. Then they softened. He straightened, stepped away from the building, and bowed slightly. "Why, ma'am, I should think she'd be delighted to have your help. But that wouldn't be for me to say. I suggest you go in there and ask her."

Louise felt herself blushing with pleasure and was instantly furious with herself. She was acting like some innocent, apple-cheeked schoolgirl, she realized. "Well, then," she managed. "In that case, I'll go in and find out for myself."

Not too long after, Taggart and Louise Thompson, standing in the open doorway of the way station, waved good-bye as the stage pulled out. The rancher, Kyle Warner, was driving, with Caroline Wells once again riding shotgun.

Before he left, Captain Farnum had promised that as soon as they reached Cheyenne and Wells Fargo learned of their plight, the agent would send out fresh horses and perhaps even armed guards, in the now unlikely event that the Sioux decided to return.

As the rumble of the stagecoach faded, Taggart squinted up at the already fierce sun, and then, shading his eyes, turned his attention to the sky over the rocks beyond the creek.

"What is it?" Louise asked.

"Buzzards," he said. "They've come to feed on them dead Indians that rancher left out there."

Louise shuddered. "How long will it take them?" she asked.

"If you mean how long to finish off them Indians, too long. I don't like it. Buzzards attract attention." He started to walk toward the one barn still standing.

"Where are you going?" she asked.

"To get a shovel."

She nodded, watched him move off for a moment, then turned and went back inside to finish cleaning up.

Miranda was still busy in the single bedroom, seeing to her husband's wound. She was having a difficult time keeping it clean, and Ty was in great discomfort, as well as being in a terrible state over the prospect of losing much of his hair. As a result, cleaning the cabin was now up to Louise.

With a sigh, she looked around her. The place was a mess, not only from the Sioux attack but from the number of people the long room had been forced to accommodate the night before. The walls were pocked with bullet holes; extra mattresses and blankets were still heaped in one corner; the pile of dishes she had already washed had yet to be put away in the cupboards above the sink; pictures that had been shattered had to be taken down from the walls, damaged furniture had to be set aside, and jagged shards of glass from the broken windows needed sweeping. Rolling up her sleeves, she lifted the wooden bucket, placed it under the sink pump, and went to work.

A half hour later, completely absorbed in her task, she discovered herself humming contentedly. When she realized why, she smiled to herself and kept right on humming.

This isolated way station at Devil's Creek, halfway

between here and nowhere, had not been her destination when she'd left Red Gap, Idaho, a week earlier. Far from it. Denver had been her eventual destination. She had sold her sporting house to one of her best girls, withdrawn her savings from the local bank, said her good-byes to all the good-time Charlies who had sworn their eternal fealty, and had set out on this journey to what she intended would be a new beginning.

She was not much over forty and was still proud of her figure. It was that of a woman, not a girl. It had the lushness that mature men appreciated, and it was only such men who interested her, for they usually had not only the wit but the wherewithal to savor the pleasures a woman with her experience and temperament could provide. She had always been pretty, perhaps beautiful, with abundant—some would say luxuriant—auburn curls, large blue eyes, and a milkmaid's complexion. But such attractions, she knew only too well, would not last forever. Each day her mortal enemy, the mirror, had warned and chided her. If she was to save herself, she had to make her move now—and so she had.

Her plan, once she reached Denver, was to open a sporting house that would cater only to the best clientele. There, surely, with such an abundance of sophisticated, wealthy men, she could not help but attract a husband or at least someone willing and eager to take care of her in a style that her talents deserved.

That, at any rate, had been her plan. Now, here she was cleaning out a two-bit way station, humming to herself because she had managed to stay behind with a frail gambler whose eyes sometimes frightened her and whom she had not known until the day before.

Shaking her head at the thought, she continued to sweep the broken window glass into a pile. She was about to reach for the dustpan when the room darkened as someone stepped into the open doorway behind her. At once she knew it could not be Dirk—his slender frame would not have blocked out the sunlight so completely. She whirled to see two men standing just inside the doorway.

She recognized them at once for what they were. Most of her adult life she had dealt with such human garbage as a matter of course—but always when she was in a position to exercise powerful authority or to grant needed favors.

Louise instantly decided they must be brothers. The one who looked older, a lean, wasted creature, fixed her with his blue eyes. As he squinted and grinned, she could see that most of his teeth were gone. He looked harmless—pathetic, even. But Louise knew better. She sensed that he had all the compassion of a rattlesnake, and was just about as harmless. Louise was even more repulsed by the sight of his younger brother, an unwashed, unshaven hulk of a man with reddish hair hanging down from under his torn, floppy-brimmed hat, and tiny green eyes that glinted in the darkened room like the shards of glass piled at her feet.

It was this second one who rubbed his face—filling the deadly silence with a raw, scratchy sound—as he stepped closer and grinned.

"Well, well, look what we got here," he said. "What's a dame with your possibles cleanin' up this place for? Last I seed you was on that stage headin' for Cheyenne. You get religion all of a sudden, maybe?"

"Leave her be, Flem," said his companion. "Can't you see, she's so pleased to see us, she cain't hardly speak. Be polite and take off your hat, fer God's sake."

"Sure, Luke, sure," the squat one said, taking off his

hat in mock obedience and stepping still closer. His smile revealed blackened stumps. Louise could smell him.

He reached out to grab her. With a quick, vicious swipe, she brought the broom handle down across his knuckles. Crying out in pain—it sounded like the squeal of a pig—he jumped back, holding his hand.

"Watch your manners!" Louise snapped. "Keep your filthy hands off me!"

"Or you'll what?" said the lean, older one, quickly moving closer and snatching the broom out of her hand.

When Louise tried to grab back the broom, the lean fellow slapped her, hard. Her head snapped around. Eyes stinging from the sudden tears, she shook her head to clear it and stepped back. "Damn you!" she breathed, her voice almost breaking. "Damn you to hell!"

"Now, now," said the fellow who had slapped her. "A lady shouldn't ought to talk like that. You mustn't be afraid of Flem and me."

"That's right," said Flem, stepping closer and baring his blackened teeth again in what he took for a smile. "We got a good look at you in Fort Laramie, woman. You ain't the type to hide your charms, and that's a fact. All you got to do now is what comes natural. So there ain't nothin' for you to be afeared of."

But it was not fear she felt, it was rage. These men were contemptible. They had her cornered, and there was nothing she could do to stop them. But she had never given it away before, and she was damned if she was going to do so now. It was more than self-preservation; it was a matter of pride.

"If either of you apes touches me," she said, her voice trembling with fury, "you'll wish you hadn't."

"Hell," Flem said. "There ain't nothin' I like better

than a chicken that flutters a mite . . . before I wring its neck, that is.''

Both men advanced on Louise. She took a quick step back and caught her foot. With a startled cry, she fell back, landing on the straw mattress. They stepped forward quickly and were looming over her, both of them licking their lips, when Miranda appeared suddenly in the bedroom doorway.

"What are you men doing?" she cried. "How *dare* you! Get away from her!"

Startled by her sudden, unexpected appearance, Flem and his brother pulled up. Through the open doorway beyond, they could see the injured stationmaster lying on the bed. "Get back in there, you old bat," Luke said, his face twisting in sudden contempt. "We'll get to you later."

"No, you won't!" snapped a sharp, cold voice from behind them.

Enormous relief flooding her, Louise glanced past the men and saw Dirk Taggart standing in the doorway, his gleaming six-gun trained on the two men. They started to turn, their hands dropping to their holsters.

But Taggart's cold voice stopped them. "Freeze, gents. The first one to go for his iron will get a hole in his back."

Both men obediently froze in their tracks. Swiftly, Louise scrambled to her feet.

"Unbuckle your gun belts, gents," Dirk told them. "And don't make any sudden moves."

Slowly, carefully, the two men did as they were told and let their gun belts drop.

As soon as the two weapons thumped to the cabin floor, Dirk said, "Pick them up, Louise, and bring them over here."

Louise swiftly plucked the gun belts and holstered

weapons off the floor and brought them to Dirk. He took both revolvers and stuck them into his belt.

"Okay, you two," Dirk said. "Turn around so I can see what a pair of human vultures look like."

The two men turned, and the withering glance they directed at Louise made her shudder. Dirk smiled.

"I guess I'm going to have to thank you," Dirk told the two men. "This way station needs horseflesh. The Sioux took our stock yesterday. Your three horses will do nicely, thank you."

"You can't take our horses," said the older one.

"What's your name, mister?"

"Luke. This here's my brother, Flem."

"Luke, I *am* going to take your horses. But I am not going to kill you. I have something else in mind."

"You better kill us," challenged Flem. "If you don't, we'll come back and break you in two."

"Don't tempt me." Dirk stepped aside. "Get outside. Now!"

As the two men slouched past Dirk and out through the door, Dirk glanced back quickly at Louise. He asked if she was all right. When Louise nodded, he told her he'd be gone for a while and that she and Miranda were to stay alert in case any more Sioux were still prowling around. Then he handed her one of the guns he had taken from the two brothers.

Standing in the doorway with Miranda a moment later, Louise watched Dirk ride out astride the big roan gelding that Kyle Warner had left behind. Ahead of him, the two brothers plodded on foot. It took some time for them to get out of sight. When she could see them no longer, she and Miranda went back inside the station house.

Louise closed the door, then slumped into one of the chairs and rested the huge revolver Dirk had given her on the table in front of her. It was over. The two men were gone. They hadn't taken her against her will. With Miranda's comforting hand resting on her shoulder, Louise began to cry softly, steadily.

It was not anger or fear that made her cry, but relief—pure, blessed relief.

Noting the tracks the fleeing Sioux had made the day before, Dirk drove his two captives in that direction. They had left the way station early that morning and it was now well past noon. The men had pleaded almost continuously to be able to stop and rest up, to take off their riding boots at least, but Dirk had steadfastly refused. When, a few hours before, with the sun pouring down upon them from almost directly overhead, they had turned in bitter fury to face him, he had simply fired carefully at the ground around their feet. The two men had spun around and continued on across the blistering landscape.

Looking around him now, noting how deep into the badlands he had driven them, Dirk pulled up. He let the two men stumble forward a few more steps before he cleared his throat and called out to them. They halted, then turned raggedly to face him.

"I figure this is far enough," Dirk said.

"You ain't gonna leave us out here without no weapons," said Luke, his voice sounding as dry as old newspaper. "You've taken our horses. Ain't that enough, you sonofabitch?"

"Don't argue with him," said Flem. "Don't give the bastard the satisfaction."

"Take off your boots," Dirk told them.

"Jesus!" said Luke.

"Now!" said Dirk.

The two men allowed themselves to collapse to the

ground. Grunting with the exertion, they tugged off their battered riding boots. Both men had suffered plenty during the long walk—riding boots were meant for stirrups, not for walking. Taggart had watched them teetering on their high, narrow heels and pointed toes, perfectly aware of the damage this was doing to their feet. And now, as the last boot was tugged free, he saw with grim satisfaction their bloodied heels and toes.

"Throw the boots over here," Dirk said.

Sullenly, the two men did as they were told.

"All right, gents," Dirk told them, "get movin'!"

"No, damn your eyes!" cried Luke. "This ain't Christian! We ain't got no weapons and no mounts. Them Sioux is out here and you know it. No white man would do this to another white man!"

"Hell. Didn't you know? I ain't no white man. I'm part Cherokee."

Both men groaned and took a painful step backward.

"Move it!" snapped Dirk. "Pick 'em up and lay 'em down!"

When they hesitated, Dirk began firing at the ground around their feet. At once the men began hopping frantically as the rounds ricocheted around their flanks. Turning swiftly, they began to hobble off.

Taggart sat on his horse patiently and watched until the two men were barely visible in the shimmering distance. Then he dismounted, picked up the bloodied boots, and climbed back up onto his horse. Without another look at the two figures dwindling on the horizon, he turned his mount and started back to the way station at Devil's Creek.

Chapter 5

As Taggart vanished in the distance, Luke sent a string of oaths after him, then turned to Flem in disgust.

"I guess maybe you saw what horse that dude was ridin'."

Flem's round, red-stubbled face grimaced. "You're damn right I saw it. A big roan gelding. Belonged to that double-crossing sonofabitch we trailed to the way station."

"Reckon that means he took the stage to Cheyenne."

"Yep. But it don't matter none. He can go clear to hell and back and we'll still get the sonofabitch. Don't you worry none about that, Luke."

"I won't. But first I'd like to go back and stomp that dude, and that juicy girl friend of his."

"We can't do it barefoot, Luke."

"I know that, dammit! I know it."

For the rest of that day, Luke and Flem struggled over the rugged land, heading for a lush, wooded benchland that seemed to hang just out of reach in the distance like a desert mirage. They reached it after nightfall and made camp in a stand of aspen beside a swift mountain stream. They didn't dare light a fire this deep in Sioux country, and without their bedrolls they shivered miserably throughout the night.

As soon as the sun showed itself above the horizon,

they set out once more, hunger clamoring insistently within them, clawing at their vitals. They had no weapons, save the single Bowie knife Flem carried. As a result, their aggravation was intensified cruelly as they glimpsed the abundant game that filled the parks and woodlands through which they trudged. The only comfort they had as the day wore on was the cool woodland shade that shielded them from the fierce sun that hung above.

The timber gave way at last to higher, more broken land. Great boulders and massive folds of rock began to dominate the landscape, and soon they were following a swift stream into a draw that widened gradually into a lush, verdant canyon. They were moving gingerly on protesting bare feet, keeping to the rocks along the side of the canyon, when a sudden thunder of horses' hooves caused them to draw back swiftly into the shadows.

They hid just in time, for just then four mounted Sioux, herding before them at least six horses, swept past them deeper into the canyon.

"Did you catch the brands on them horses?" Flem asked.

"I did," replied Luke, grinning wolfishly at his brother. "Looks like we done found the braves that robbed that way station."

Flem nodded, took out his Bowie, and began to sharpen it against his palm. "Yes sir," he said, grinning. "We done found them redskins *and* the horses they took. Looks like we're done walkin'."

Luke's spirits had risen a notch, too. Like his brother, he would have been willing to steal horses from the Devil himself if it meant he no longer had to travel on foot. "We'll find their camp and take them tonight," he said.

Flem didn't bother to respond. He simply continued

to drag the blade of his knife rapidly back and forth across his rough palm.

It was a little before midnight.

The Indians had set up camp at the edge of the stream that wound through the canyon. The stolen horses had been herded onto a small grassy sward close to the canyon wall. A single Sioux warrior was guarding them. Another Indian was on sentry duty in the rocks above the camp, sitting cross-legged on a narrow ledge just above the horses. The two remaining braves were asleep beside the smoldering campfire.

The moon, as bright and shiny as a new silver dollar, was balanced neatly on the rim of the canyon just behind Luke. It gave him, poised just above the Indian on the ledge, all the light he needed. Below him in the canyon, the Sioux guarding the horses was clearly visible, his dark shoulders shining dully in the moonlight.

Luke stood up.

Showing himself in this manner was the agreed-upon signal that would send Flem against the Indian guarding the horses. A club grasped in his right hand, Luke stood poised against the bright night sky for a couple of seconds longer to make sure Flem saw him. Then he jumped.

He landed on the ledge lightly enough, just behind the sentry, but the Indian heard him. The Sioux's buffalo-tooth necklace gleamed in the moonlight as he sprang to his feet and whirled around. It was too late. Luke was already bringing down his club. He felt it crunch through the Indian's skull. Dropping the club, he reached out and caught the Sioux's rifle as the dead warrior dropped silently to the floor of the ledge.

Luke glanced down at the horses.

They were moving restlessly but were still reasonably quiet. The Indian guarding them was no longer visible.

Swiftly climbing down off the ledge, Luke approached the nearest of the two sleeping Indians. He was within ten feet of him when he saw Flem's dark figure rushing through the gloom toward the Indian on the other side of the campfire. Luke saw his brother pause over the sleeping Indian, then caught the gleam of Flem's blade a second before he plunged it into the still form huddled at his feet. Again and again Flem plunged his blade home. Luke could hear his brother panting from the exertion. But the fatally wounded Indian did not die quietly. He uttered a sudden, shattering cry.

Luke's Indian sat up and turned in time to see Luke sweeping through the night toward him.

For a split second the Sioux's dark eyes and Luke's met as the Indian sprang from under his blanket, a dagger in his dark hand. Swinging his rifle like a club, Luke caught the brave in the side. The Indian went down, and Luke swung the rifle butt a second time, crunching through the Indian's temple. As the Indian's body began to twitch in death, Luke spun away and saw Flem on the other side of the campfire, wiping his blade across his thigh.

"That's the lot of them," Flem said.

"Looks like it."

A loud cry punctured the sudden stillness.

Both men turned to see the Indian whom Flem had supposedly killed earlier rush at the horses, knocking down the rope corral as he did so. As the Sioux leaped astride the nearest horse, the rest reared in panic and immediately plunged ahead of him down the canyon.

Uttering an oath, Flem flung his knife. The spinning blade winked in the moonlight a split second before it buried itself in the fleeing Sioux's back. The Indian threw both hands in the air and peeled back off his horse.

But the damage was done. The two men would have a long walk ahead of them before they caught up to those spooked mounts. Luke examined his rifle. As he had suspected the moment he first hefted it, it was empty. Searching further, he and his brother found only two more rifles in the camp, both empty as well, with not a single round to be found anywhere.

"I'm thinking we better get after them horses," Flem said. "They shouldn't get far in this canyon—not this time of night."

"We hope," Luke said. "Thing is, they could run into something in the dark—hurt themselves. Just what we need now."

Without replying, Flem disappeared into the shadows to retrieve his Bowie knife.

Luke dropped the rifle he had taken, then went down on one knee beside the Sioux he had just killed. The dead warrior was still holding the dagger he had drawn. Carefully, Luke peeled back the Sioux's fingers, then stood up with the weapon, inspecting it closely. It was nothing more than a pointed stick, still smoldering from the campfire from which the Indian had plucked it. Luke tossed it to the ground in disgust.

Despite the bloodied corpses crumpled in the darkness behind him, and the fact that he was weaponless, a smirking smile crept onto Luke's face as he hurried after his brother. They'd catch up to them mounts soon enough. With horseflesh under them, they'd be able to return to the Devil's Creek way station. There'd be food there—and a vengeance that would be even sweeter.

Early the next afternoon, Kyle hauled back on the reins of his weary team as the stagecoach pulled up in front of the Wells Fargo & Co. express office in Cheyenne.

Because of its late arrival, news of its coming had spread from the moment it had been sighted entering Cheyenne. Long before Kyle reached the express office, excited queries had been hurled up at him from the sidewalks. His straightforward replies had electrified the townsmen. Not only had highwaymen tried to rob the gold that the stage carried, but Sioux had attacked the way station at Devil's Creek and run off all the horses. This sensational news ignited the townsmen.

A large, excited crowd was waiting in the street in front of the express office. As soon as the horses pulled up, the citizens of Cheyenne surged around the stage, making it almost impossible for Kyle and Caroline to descend from the box. The questions came at them and at the passengers so hard and fast that it was all any of them could do to answer. Fortunately, as soon as word spread about the two wounded men inside the coach, help was immediately forthcoming.

A doctor pushed through the crowd to see to the wounded, and on his heels came a hearty, apple-cheeked woman in her late forties who insisted that the wounded men be taken to her rooming house. It was obvious that this woman—her name was Sarah Crouse—knew both Tim Moody and Seth. The doctor, after a quick examination of Moody's wound, agreed to have the Jehu taken to her rooming house and, turning to the crowd, sought assistance in transporting the wounded men there.

Almost at once, makeshift stretchers were brought, and even though Seth insisted that he could make it to Sarah Crouse's place on foot, he was overruled and made to lie back on one of the stretchers as the townsmen bore him and Tim Moody off. Sarah Crouse's hospitality extended to Caroline, Mary Beth, and Kyle as well. Caroline and Mary Beth accepted gratefully, but Kyle thanked the woman and declined.

As Tim Moody and Seth were carried off, they took a few of the crowd with them. Kyle, doing his best to ignore the persistent questions of those still clustered around the stage, pushed his way through the crowd and found refuge in the relative quiet of the express office.

But as he stood inside, waiting for the Wells Fargo agent to finish seeing to the unloading of the stage, he glanced through the window and saw the difficulty Captain Farnum was experiencing as he attempted to escort Santoro to the local jail. The news of the Sioux attack on the way station had inflamed Cheyenne's citizens. The fact that Santoro was an Apache, not a Sioux, seemed to make little difference to these men. To them, one Indian was very much like any other—and all were ready targets for their outrage.

Deciding he could speak to the station agent later, Kyle hurried from the office, bulled his way through the crowd, and mounted the wooden sidewalk alongside Farnum and the Apache just in time to fling a drunk off Santoro. The boozed-up townsman had grabbed Santoro's long hair and was attempting to scalp the Indian without the aid of a knife—to the roaring approval of the growing crowd.

The response to Kyle's action was unfavorable, with most of the crowd shouting obscenities, accusing Kyle of being an Indian lover. But Captain Farnum appeared grateful for Kyle's help, and together the two men hustled the Apache through the crowd and into the arms of the local sheriff and his deputy, who had been on their way to help. A moment later, the four men had safely escorted Santoro to the sheriff's office and into the cellblock in back.

As Kyle watched the sheriff turn the key in the lock of

the cell door, he glanced past him at Santoro. Just behind the bars, the Apache stood with his arms folded, watching them. Santoro had not uttered a word as they hustled him through the crowd and into this cell, but as Kyle looked into the Apache's eyes, he sensed the desperation—perhaps even the wild, animal terror—that must have gripped the Indian the moment that barred door clanged shut behind him.

Kyle had never been imprisoned, but he thought he understood perfectly what it must be like for Santoro. One winter, Kyle had found a trap where a beaver had chewed through his own leg to free himself. At that moment, Santoro didn't look any less desperate than that beaver must have been when he gnawed away his limb.

The tough part of it was that once again—just as at the way station and during the stage ride to Cheyenne—Kyle didn't dare say anything to Santoro with the captain at his elbow. All he could do was hope that Santoro understood that, although Kyle had done little to free him thus far, it was only a matter of time before he acted.

"Let's go, Kyle," said the captain. "I owe you a drink. You, too, Sheriff."

"My pleasure," said Kyle, following the captain through the door.

The sheriff's name was Miles Bounty. After handing his deputy a loaded shotgun, he and Kyle followed the captain as he shouldered his way through the crowd and crossed the street to Frenchy's Saloon.

But Kyle left the two men at the entrance to the saloon with a promise to join them later, then returned to the express office and gave the somewhat anxious Wells Fargo agent a complete report on what had happened at the Devil's Creek way station. He reported on the condition of Ty Wilks and finished up by reminding him forcefully that two Wells Fargo passengers had volunteered to remain behind at Devil's Creek to help the stationmaster and his wife.

The fellow was suitably impressed and promised to send out fresh horses to the way station along with a contingent of well-armed men as soon as he could round them up. Satisfied, Kyle left the office and headed back to Frenchy's.

When he arrived at the saloon, he found the sheriff and the captain at a small table in the rear, drinking quietly. The crowd in front of the sheriff's lockup, Kyle noticed, had grown considerably by this time. As he sat down at the table, he glanced at the sheriff and apprised him of this fact.

"Hell, Kyle," the big, bluff man said. "I know that crowd is growing. I can *hear* as well as see."

Finishing his whiskey, Sheriff Bounty pushed the empty glass from him and stood up wearily. "Guess I'll go see if I can dig up the town constable and a few more deputies. Looks like I'll be needin' them before this night is over." He fixed the captain with his deep-set eyes. "This Apache's your prisoner, Captain. I'm assuming I can count on your help as well."

"You can."

Sheriff Bounty pulled his battered Stetson down more firmly onto his head, then strode from the saloon.

As the sheriff disappeared through the batwing doors of the saloon, Kyle glanced across the small table at Farnum. "What is it, Captain? Why have you come so far to bring back a single Apache chieftain?"

The captain studied Kyle's face for a moment, obviously deliberating whether Kyle had any right to the particulars of Santoro's case. Then, with a weary shrug, he said, "That single Apache chieftain is responsible for the

74

massacre of a settler, his wife, and three children. In addition, Warner, he's a renegade, having fled from the reservation. In short, he's a fugitive as well as a murderer."

"I don't believe you, Captain."

The captain finished his whiskey, then eyed Kyle narrowly. "What don't you believe?"

"That this Apache killed the settler and his family."

"I don't care if you believe it or not, Warner. But all available evidence points to him and the four other Apache who left the reservation with him. The settler was robbed of his horses and a great deal of provisions—precisely what a fleeing band of Apache would need."

"Is that all the evidence you can point to?"

"There was one more thing," the captain said dryly.

"And what was that?"

"The way the man and his wife and three children were killed—or rather, the manner of their deaths and subsequent mutilations. It revealed the fine hand of the Apache with all their satanic inventiveness—their awful, studied brutality. I was there when the bodies were found, Warner. No hand but that of an Apache savage could possibly have been responsible for that horror."

"That doesn't mean that this chieftain was responsible. It could have been any party of Apache. Or white men bent on robbing those settlers and mutilating their victims to implicate the Apache."

"Yes, I suppose it could have been other Apache or, as you suggest, white marauders attempting to pass the blame on to the Apache. But, you see, this fellow Santoro has already admitted leading his braves through that settler's land—and also taking from him what supplies he and his band needed."

Kyle felt slightly sick. "And did he admit to killing the settler and his family as well?"

"No. But he only admitted what he did because I found him astride one of the settler's horses. Still, I'm not worried. Once I have him before a military court, the entire truth of this ugly business will come out. Then I shall see this Apache hang. Further, I will see to it that his many tribesmen on the reservation are brought in to witness his execution."

Kyle was somewhat taken aback by the captain's revelations. Still, despite the weight of evidence, he couldn't get himself to believe that Santoro had indeed done what the captain alleged. There had to be a better explanation than the one Farnum accepted so eagerly.

Before moving north to Montana, Kyle and his family had settled in New Mexico during the Apache uprising in 1861, when Cochise was unjustly arrested for kidnapping, then escaped and led his warriors on a trail of terror through the Southwest. Kyle had seen the Apache as a warrior, firsthand. Indeed, it was through just such an action as the captain had described that he had first met Santoro.

While on their way to their ranch one day, he and his father had been surprised and surrounded by a small war party led by the young Santoro. No sooner had his father halted than the Indians pulled him from the wagon seat and began pummeling him unmercifully, their delighted cries shattering the grim desert silence. Outraged, the young Kyle threw all caution to the wind and flung himself upon the leader of the war party. So furious and so unexpected was his attack that he managed to wrest Santoro's war club from him, and was in the act of bringing it down upon the hapless chieftain when the other Apache—laughing uproariously at Santoro's discomfiture—dragged Kyle off him.

Although he and his father had expected only a

fearsome death as the certain reward for the boy's behavior, in true Apache fashion Santoro rewarded such courage by mingling his blood with Kyle's and proclaiming the boy to be a blood brother and forever under his protection.

And so, under Santoro's protective wing, Kyle and his family were able to remain, unmolested, in Apache country.

"What's your interest in this Indian, Warner?" the captain asked, waving one of the bar girls over to his table. "You seem to have a lot more at stake than you're lettin' on." The captain peered closely at Kyle. "You wouldn't happen to know this Apache, would you?"

"As a matter of fact, I do know him. That is, I saw him on more than one occasion when my family lived in New Mexico some years ago."

"I thought so," said the captain. He turned to the bar girl and ordered another round. Looking back at Kyle, he said, "Well then, you also know that my estimate of the Apache is not at all out of line."

"Yes," Kyle admitted, somewhat reluctantly. "I suppose so. But I've known Apache I would be proud to call my friends."

"Have you? I am afraid that I cannot echo your noble sentiments, Warner. To me, the Apache represents a barbarism that must be stamped out completely if the West is to be made safe for civilized folks." The captain looked shrewdly at Kyle. "Tell me, why did your people move out of New Mexico?"

"My mother," Kyle replied ruefully. "She was afraid of the Apache."

Captain Farnum leaned back in his chair. "I rest my case," he said, an ironic gleam in his dark eyes.

Kyle was content to let it go at that for the moment and said nothing more on the subject as their drinks arrived. Before they had a chance to raise their glasses, however, the steadily increasing crowd noise from the street changed suddenly to a series of shattering roars.

Gulping down their whiskey, both men hurried from the saloon and saw that the crowd—which now completely filled the street—had produced a leather-lunged partisan who was haranguing the citizens of Cheyenne with great effectiveness. To hear him tell it, the death of this single Apache in the jail behind him was the only thing that could give all of them back their manhood. If they let this Apache live, on the other hand, they would be nothing more than spineless cowards, unworthy of the respect and love of decent men and women.

Even as this man whipped the crowd into a lather, one of its members pushed his way onto the sidewalk beside him, brandishing a coil of rope, the hangman's knot already tied. As this fellow raised the noose over his head, another exultant roar broke from the crowd. Kyle could almost taste the bloodlust in the air.

"Looks like a necktie party coming up," he commented.

"Not if I can help it," replied the captain. He glanced sharply at Kyle. "You helped out back there. You still willing to lend a hand?"

Kyle nodded. "Count me in."

The captain looked back at the crowd, disdain etched on his handsome face. "These bravos won't make any moves until it gets dark, I'm thinking," he said. "And not until they get a little more whiskey under their belts. So we've got time to make ready. I'm going across the street to see how much luck the sheriff is having digging up those extra deputies."

"All right. I'll join you later. I'm going to hunt up that rooming house where they took Tim Moody and the express messenger."

The captain's smile was barely perceptible as he said, "And Miss Caroline Wells."

Kyle smiled in spite of himself. "Yes," he said. "And Caroline Wells."

"Give her my regards, Warner," the captain said, as he stepped off the boardwalk and shouldered his way into the crowd.

Caroline Wells had not remained long at Sarah Crouse's boardinghouse. As soon as she had bathed and changed, she read over once again the letter her brother had sent her six months before. Then, after checking on the condition of the stage driver and Seth Loman, she hurried from the boardinghouse in search of one Brian Wallace, mentioned in her brother's letter as the owner and proprietor of a freight company where her brother was working as a freight handler and general roustabout.

Sarah Crouse had given Caroline directions. The Wallace Freight Company, she said, was located on the other side of the railroad tracks, across from the new train depot. It consisted of a huge warehouse and stable that were still being built. Now, as Caroline hurried along the crowded streets, she understood why the freight company was, as Sarah Crouse had said, still abuilding.

All this ceaseless activity, this choking plenitude of men, was due to the Union Pacific, which was in a desperate hurry to stretch its tracks ever westward and needed these men to accomplish that stupendous task. So here they were, swarming past her on all sides. Some men were dressed so handsomely that it seemed they had just stepped off the train from the East, while others were so poorly and carelessly attired, so blatantly and brazenly unkempt, that she was offended. They were noisy and boisterous, most of them, and it seemed to Caroline that every single one of them was either entering or leaving a saloon.

In all her life, she had never seen so many saloons, taverns, and gambling halls in one place. Glancing inside a few of them as she passed, she could not help but notice the women who worked in these establishments—and shudder. Some of the saloons were handsome, glittering palaces with bands playing even now, in the middle of the afternoon. But such places were the exception, not the rule. The majority of the saloons and gambling halls were dim, dour tunnels, crowded and noisy, the only music the coyotelike yapping of the drunken men brawling within. And each place stank of corruption.

Caroline thought of Louise Thompson then, and shook her head in wonder that a woman with such qualities could have spent her working years in places like that and still retain—as Louise undoubtedly had—a certain beauty, even strength. Louise Thompson must be a very tough woman, it appeared. Very tough indeed.

When it came time to cross Fifteenth Street to get to the train depot, Caroline almost lost her courage. The dusty street was clogged with wagons loaded with telegraph poles, steel rails, railroad ties, and other supplies of all kinds. The teamsters driving the huge wagons seemed unwilling to recognize the presence of anyone on foot. They filled the air with ear-blistering curses and the crack of their uncoiling whips. Twice Caroline attempted to make it across, only to dart back to the wooden sidewalk as heavily laden wagons, pulled along by towering Belgian workhorses, threatened to run her down. But at last she made it, her heart thumping wildly as she reached the other side.

As Caroline crossed the tracks, she found herself in another world, a rabbit warren of narrow streets and filthy alleys lined with tarpaper shacks and tents. At the same time, she was struck by the number of Orientals she now saw on all sides of her, their heads down as they hurried along in a kind of steady, untiring dogtrot. Their faces reflected no emotion, it appeared, and they seemed eager not to meet her eyes. They were strangers—unwelcome strangers—in a distant land. She could almost feel their loneliness, the sad isolation through which they hurried.

When she reached the freight company warehouse, a single inquiry brought her to the company's office. She entered quietly and found herself in a cluttered room, standing alongside a clerk wearing a green eyeshade. The clerk was sitting on a tall stool, poring over what appeared to be hundreds of bills of lading. When she cleared her throat, the clerk glanced up with such startled suddenness that he almost fell from his stool.

"I'm sorry," Caroline said. "I didn't mean to startle you."

The clerk grinned apologetically. "I get lost in all these bills of lading, ma'am," he said, hurriedly putting down his pen. "We sure are busy."

"So I see. Is Mr. Wallace in?"

"Yes, he is, ma'am," the clerk said. "Follow me."

The clerk led Caroline from his office deeper into the warehouse, past stacks of great wooden crates and finally to a much larger, glassed-in office tucked into the farthest corner of the building. As the clerk opened the door for her and stepped back to let her enter ahead of him, she could smell the new wood that had only recently been used in the construction of the office.

The man she assumed to be Brian Wallace was standing in front of a tall file cabinet. He had turned as the door opened. As Caroline stepped into his office, he slammed shut the file drawer and advanced toward them. "Yes, Bill, what is it?"

"Mr. Wallace," said the clerk, "this woman wants to see you."

Brian Wallace nodded curtly to Caroline, then glanced back at the clerk. "Thanks, Bill."

The young man vanished out the door. Wallace indicated a chair by his desk with a sweep of his meaty hand.

"Won't you sit down, ma'am?" he asked.

"Thank you," Caroline said.

Brian Wallace was a powerfully built fellow with broad shoulders and a round, beefy face. A quizzical frown remained on his face as Caroline sat down in the chair by his desk.

"This is a pleasure, ma'am," he said, slumping into his own seat behind the desk. "What can I do for you?"

"I am looking for Everett Wells, Mr. Wallace."

The frown left Wallace's face—to be replaced by a look almost of dismay. "Everett?" he repeated. "Now what would you be wanting with the likes of him, ma'am?"

"You know him?"

"I guess I could say that."

"He worked for you, didn't he?"

"That was some time ago, ma'am. You ain't answered my question. Why do you want Everett?" His eyes narrowed in sudden suspicion. "He ain't made no trouble for you, has he?"

"Everett Wells is my brother, Mr. Wallace."

Wallace's florid face lost its color so swiftly that Caroline was startled. "My God," the man breathed, looking more closely at Caroline. "I should've noticed the likeness. I'm sorry, Miss Wells."

"If you can help me find my brother, Mr. Wallace, I

will be very grateful. He hasn't written for six months. I must find him—our father is a very sick man.''

Wallace got quickly to his feet. His agitation was quite pronounced as he looked down almost despairingly at Caroline. "I am sorry, Miss Wells," he told her, "but there's nothing I can do for you. Your brother hasn't worked for me for at least five months.''

"You mean he's left Cheyenne?''

"I'm sure I don't know, Miss Wells—or care. And if you had any sense, you'd give up trying to find your brother. He's a big boy now—able to make his own mistakes, *and* take the consequences. My advice to you is to get back to your sick father and forget all about that brother of yours.''

"Mr. Wallace," Caroline said, "why did my brother leave your employ?''

The man hesitated. For a moment it looked as if he was about to tell her. Then he shook his head decisively. "I'd rather not say," he replied finally.

With that, he strode to the door and pulled it open.

"I'm very busy, Miss Wells," he told her. "Now, if you don't mind . . .''

"Please, Mr. Wallace," Caroline pleaded, getting to her feet. "You must help me find my brother. It's not for myself that I'm asking.''

"I'm sorry, Miss Wells, but I cannot help you. And now, you *must* excuse me. I have a great deal of work to do.''

Caroline walked past the man and out of his office. This man was not telling her the truth. He could help her, but he was willfully refusing to do so. She was suddenly furious. As Wallace was closing the door on her, she turned and confronted him. "If you won't help me," she told him fiercely, "I'll find someone who will!''

Wallace seemed as distraught as Caroline was. "Miss Wells," he pleaded with her. "I beg of you. *Please*. Forget your brother. Go back home to your father!"

He hurriedly pulled the door shut and swiftly moved back to his desk.

For a moment Caroline stood outside the door, staring in bewilderment and anger through the glass at Brian Wallace. Then, with hot, scalding tears streaming down her face, she stumbled back through the warehouse and out into the street. She was convinced that something terrible had happened to her brother, and that this man Wallace was responsible.

Chapter 6

Mary Beth sat quietly in the corner of the darkened room, watching over the restless, sleeping form of Tim Moody.

She and Sarah Crouse had assisted the doctor when he went in after the bullet that was lodged in the stage driver's shoulder. First they had poured whiskey down his throat, after which she and Sarah had done their best to hold Moody down while the doctor dug the bullet out of his shoulder. The doctor had had a devil of a time finding the slug. Then, after the bullet had been retrieved, a terrifying freshet of blood had followed it out, and for a few frantic moments the three of them had almost despaired of being able to stanch the flow.

Tim Moody groaned and turned his head. At once, Mary Beth left her chair and hurried to the man's side. He was waving his right arm, his fist clenched, both eyes closed. She bent close and was almost knocked out by the powerful stench of the whiskey on his breath. He groaned again and turned his head away from her, his eyes remaining tightly closed. Then he dropped his right arm and began to snore.

Straightening, Mary Beth watched him a moment longer, then turned wearily and went back to her chair. Although the man was still suffering from the effects of the operation—and all that whiskey—he certainly seemed to be tough enough to survive all he had been through. She was confident that he would live.

If he survives the whiskey, that is, she thought to herself grimly.

Mrs. Crouse had drawn the curtains to keep out the sunlight, but enough broke through to bathe Mary Beth in a warm, golden glow. In better times and under different circumstances, she might have been called a strikingly beautiful woman, with features as delicate and clean as those of a Dresden doll. But at the moment, Mary Beth looked considerably older than her thirty-four years. Her shoulders were hunched and narrow, her face and figure emaciated. Already, her blond hair was streaked with gray, her cheeks were sunken, and her hazel eyes peered out of dark hollows.

As she sat there staring at the restless form before her, she tried once again to understand what had happened to all the fine hopes and dreams that had filled her childhood, and especially to that dream of marriage and a family of her own, with its warm fires and contentment. And her dream of love. What had become of that?

So certain had she been that she would be happy with Amos, so much in love with him had she been, that she had disobeyed her parents' wishes and run off with him when she was only seventeen. Oh, how exciting it had been! The strength of his arms around her, the smell of him, the floodgates of passion his kisses had released within her!

And yet, even during those first heady, tumultuous days, she had begun to notice in her lover indications of what later became a dismaying loutishness—in addition to a lamentable lack of foresight and good sense. Indeed, it was this last failing that had doomed his first enterprise, the operation of a grain mill. Then, after a series of disastrous attempts at farming that reduced them each time to fearsome poverty, Amos had dragged her west for a new start—only to repeat his earlier failures.

Meanwhile, not content with being just a poor provider, he became a brute as well, at times beating her unmercifully. At first he turned on her only after he had been drinking, and she had been inclined to blame it on that. But he soon found other excuses to vent his rage, until at last he would turn on her whenever he felt the need to release his frustrations.

By this time she no longer loved her husband—she loathed and feared him. She had to force herself to endure his unwanted caresses. Yet, since by this time she had already given birth to Caleb, she knew she was bound to this man for the rest of her life—as the minister who had married them said, "For better or for worse—until death do you part." Therefore, she had no choice but to make the best of her life with Amos, to thank the good Lord for whatever blessings came her way, and not to complain unduly if things didn't always go as she wanted.

But at the same time that she came to this realization, Mary Beth came to another decision as well. She would have no more children by this man—not unless he changed for the better. And of course he didn't, which meant that her efforts to keep Amos from her bed during her more fertile periods only infuriated him, intensifying the rage he now seemed to carry with him constantly.

Having endured his brutishness and his inability to provide for her and her son, she soon had to endure his blatant infidelities as well. It was at about this time that a stubborn inner voice began prompting her to put aside tiny sums and hide them where her husband couldn't find them. At first, she wasn't entirely sure why, but the thought of that growing cache of money in the corner of her dresser drawer comforted her, kept her going.

This past year, locusts had devastated their only crop, and Amos had been forced to rustle cattle from a neighboring rancher in order to feed his family through the winter. A week ago that rancher and his foreman had visited their farm and warned Amos that if he touched any more of his beef, Amos would have to answer to him for it. The rancher had left no doubt in their minds what measures he was prepared to take.

Amos's response—later, when the two men had ridden off—had been to turn on Mary Beth and beat her unmercifully. The pretext he used was her plea that he not go against that rancher again, even if it meant moving on. The beating had been particularly brutal, with a mean thoroughness that left little to chance.

Later that same day, as she struggled through supper, trying not to notice her partially closed eye and the constant ache in her rib cage, she came to her decision. She could not—she *would* not—live with this man any longer. He would soon be an outlaw, if he was not one already. Her private cache had grown to almost fifty dollars. With it, she would escape from this man's cruel bondage and return to her parents in Springfield, Massachusetts.

The moment she allowed this thought to express itself, she felt herself fill with a sudden, intoxicating elation. She felt as a prisoner might who had just seen the prison gates swing wide.

Glancing across the table at her husband, she saw him bent over his plate, stuffing an already full mouth, gravy running down his chin. Then she heard his belch—a loud, disgusting sound that filled the small cabin. He glanced up at her and met her gaze, obviously enjoying her discomfort; he knew only too well how much she hated it when he did that. Still smirking, he ducked his head and resumed shoveling the food into his mouth. Watching him, she realized with a shock how much of an animal he had become—with none of an animal's natural grace or cleanliness.

She turned to her twelve-year-old son. He was a good boy, she realized, but he was already becoming like his father, if not in his features, certainly in his mannerisms, in his piggish behavior. Her heart ached at the thought of leaving him—but she had no choice. How could she possibly take him with her? He would not go. He would not leave his father.

She went back to her food, ducking her head so that neither of them could see the tears that had suddenly welled in her eyes the moment she realized she was going to have to leave her son behind.

Now, thinking back to that fateful day, Mary Beth found it impossible to imagine what else she could have done under the circumstances. But if that were so—and surely it was—why did she find it so impossible to quiet the constant ache, the deep melancholy that would not leave her, day or night?

Tim Moody stirred again, suddenly raising his good arm high, only to let it drop heavily. Mary Beth was on her feet instantly, again hovering over him anxiously. But the man was still unconscious, still wrestling with whatever demons lived within his soul.

Mary Beth shuddered at the thought. Were there demons fastened to her soul as well? Was that why she had allowed herself to abandon her son as she had? Was she indeed a wicked, evil woman, as Amos maintained? And what would become of her now? That paltry fifty dollars—a sum that had looked so enormous when she had first counted it—was already reduced to little more than a pittance. And without money, what would become of her?

A pounding on the front door of the rooming house cut into her thoughts. She turned away from Tim Moody and hurried across the room as the furious pounding continued. Pulling open the bedroom door, she watched as a very red-faced and angry Sarah Crouse, her hands trembling with fury, yanked open the front door.

When Mary Beth saw who it was at the door, she almost collapsed.

Amos was standing in the doorway—and beside him stood her son, Caleb. Amos's face was as raw with fury as Mrs. Crouse's was. Her heart thudding in her chest like that of a wild animal, Mary Beth pulled back swiftly so that she could not be seen from the doorway, and watched as Amos confronted Mrs. Crouse.

"You Sarah Crouse?" he barked.

"That's right," Sarah answered, her voice just as heavy. "And just who in blazes might *you* be?"

"I'm Mary Beth's husband, and this here's her boy. We come to take her home—where she belongs!"

"Now, hold it right there, buster!" Sarah said, planting herself firmly in the open door. "No one invited you in here! So you just simmer down and learn to say *please*."

Mary Beth held her breath in horror. Sarah Crouse was not a small woman; she was five-feet-four or -five, broad of beam, with a round, cheery face. Even so, Amos towered over her, a look of black rage on his face. At any moment Mary Beth expected her husband to strike out with the fury of a thunderbolt—to smote Sarah for her impertinence in blocking his way.

Instead, she witnessed a miracle.

Amos backed up. He appeared flustered. His face

fell. For a moment it looked as if he were going to cry. Then he stammered, "But I know she's in there!"

"You stay right where you are," Sarah demanded. "I'll see if she wants to see you."

With that she stepped back and swung the door shut on Amos, then hurried over to Mary Beth, standing in the bedroom doorway. "Is that man your husband?" she demanded.

"Yes, he is."

"Do you want to see him?"

"No, not him. But . . . but my son, Caleb, is with him. . . ." Mary Beth was in an agony of indecision. She didn't want to have anything to do with Amos, but her son was a different matter entirely.

"And you want to see Caleb," the big woman prompted gently.

"Yes."

"Then you'll have to see your husband."

Mary Beth nodded.

"Go into the sitting room. I'll show him in."

"Sarah, would you . . . stay with me?"

"If you want." Then she frowned slightly and glanced past Mary Beth at the sleeping Tim Moody. "How's Tim?"

"He's still asleep."

She nodded. "All right. I'll show your husband in."

Mary Beth hurried into the sitting room. It was a dim, heavily furnished room with upholstered chairs and two sofas. Mary Beth sat down on one of the sofas. If she wasn't standing, she felt, Amos couldn't possibly feel threatened. In that case, perhaps he wouldn't feel called upon to strike her. Maybe then they could discuss matters in a more civilized manner.

But the moment she saw Amos stalk into the room

with Caleb, she realized what a forlorn hope that was. Sarah Crouse followed after them, closing the sliding doors as soon as Amos and Caleb were inside. Sarah then swiftly moved over to the sofa and positioned herself beside Mary Beth. Before she knew what she was doing, Mary Beth reached up and took Sarah's hand. Sarah squeezed Mary Beth's hand reassuringly.

His confidence back in full, Amos pulled up directly in front of the two women, feet planted wide, his dark eyes burning with indignation. For a fleeting moment, Mary Beth wished that Dirk Taggart, that gambler who had saved her in Fort Laramie, were at hand.

"Come home, Mary Beth," Amos commanded. "Your son needs you."

"And you," Mary Beth asked, her voice quavering. "What about you, Amos?"

"Dammit to hell!" the man thundered. "I need you, too!"

"That . . . that wasn't a very nice way to say it, Amos."

"Nice way! Thunderation, woman! Do you want me to go down on my knees to you? You're the one that done wrong! You're the one that run away. You're lucky I'm willin' to take you back. You know what I had to do to catch up to you? Why, Caleb and I rode near night and day through Sioux country to get here in time. Now you stop this nonsense and come back with us!"

Mary Beth felt defeated. She looked wearily at Caleb. "Son," she said, "is that what you want, too?"

The boy moistened dry lips. He appeared ready to burst into tears at any moment. He tried to speak out, but couldn't. All he could manage was a desperate, quick nod.

Tears suddenly welling in her eyes, Mary Beth opened her arms to the boy. With a cry, he rushed into them.

Hugging him to her, Mary Beth rocked back and forth. The boy's choking sobs caused her own body to shudder as well and made her hug him all the harder. At last, the boy's sobs diminished. Still with her arms around Caleb, Mary Beth glanced up at her husband.

He was looking down at the two of them, his face still hard, still unrelenting. But worse than that was the ugly look of triumph that distorted his unshaven, brutal face. She knew then why he had brought the boy with him. With cold calculation, he had known full well the effect Caleb would have on her.

Slowly, Mary Beth pushed Caleb away from her and kissed him on his forehead. Then she brushed back a lock of his unruly hair. "Go back to your father, Caleb," she said.

Amos frowned suddenly. "Well, are you comin', wife?"

"No," Mary Beth said, her voice surprisingly firm. "Not now."

"What do you mean, not now?"

"I don't know. But not now. I'm not ready yet."

"Damn you, woman!" Amos cried, moving a step closer. "You're coming with me and you're comin' now!"

But when he reached down to grab Mary Beth, Sarah knocked away his hand and placed her impressive bulk between them. "Don't you dare touch this woman!" she cried. "Not in my house! I'll have the law on you! Sheriff Bounty is a good friend of mine and he's got a jail he don't mind fillin' with the likes of you!"

Startled, Amos pulled back. Then, his face glowering murderously, he pulled himself up to his full height. "All right! All right! I'm leavin' this time, Mary Beth! But Caleb and I'll be waitin' for you at the Cheyenne Rest. If you don't come to your senses soon, I'm comin' after you!''

At that moment the doors to the sitting room slid back. Kyle Warner and Caroline Wells were standing in the doorway. It was Kyle who spoke first.

''What's all the shouting in here?'' he asked. Then, noting the threatening attitude of Amos and his proximity to the two women, his eyes narrowed in suspicion. ''Are you women all right?'' he asked.

''Yes,'' Sarah Crouse said emphatically. ''Now that you're here, mister. This here gentleman with the loud voice was just leavin'.'' Sarah looked back at Amos. ''Ain't that right, mister?''

Without replying, Amos grabbed Caleb's hand and stalked from the room, dragging his son after him. A moment later, the front door slammed shut behind him with such force that the room shuddered. Sarah sagged down on the sofa beside Mary Beth. Shaking her head, she reached out and took the young woman's hands in hers.

''That's some man you married, dearie—a real winner.''

Mary Beth was too upset to reply. Fighting back her tears, she jumped to her feet and hurried from the room. Entering the bedroom, she closed the door firmly behind her, then hurried over to check the stage driver's condition. He was tossing restlessly but was still asleep.

She moved back to her chair in the corner, and only then, her handkerchief muffling her sobs, did she allow the tears to come.

Kyle Warner and Caroline Wells remained standing in the middle of the sitting room as Mary Beth rushed past them into the bedroom. Kyle was deeply affected by the woman's grief, and for some reason it seemed to draw him closer to Caroline. She seemed to sense this as well.

"Let's sit over there," Caroline said softly, indicating the sofa.

As they sat down, Mrs. Crouse said, "I'm going into the bedroom and see how Tim's doing." She sighed. "And maybe I can give that poor woman some comfort."

As the big woman left, Kyle turned to Caroline. The two had met only minutes before on the boardinghouse steps. Looking into her eyes at that time, Kyle was almost certain he had seen panic. It was obvious that she had a great need to confide in him.

"Now, young lady," Kyle said, his voice gentle. "What's wrong? Seems to me there's something bothering you. A few minutes ago, outside on the steps, I got the feelin' you were mightily upset about something."

Caroline nodded wearily. "Yes," she admitted. "I was—I *am*—upset. But now, when I see what Mary Beth has to contend with . . ." She shuddered. "My trouble is bad enough, but all I can think of now is poor Beth. . . ."

With surprising ease, Kyle put his arm around Caroline's shoulder and pulled her closer to him. "I know," he said softly. "That jasper she married sure is no bargain."

Caroline let her head rest on Kyle's shoulder.

It happened so naturally that it took a moment for Kyle to notice and feel the wonder of it. No doubt it was those long miles they had spent together on the stagecoach driver's box, talking little as they leaned together on the curves and braced themselves as one whenever the road ahead threatened. During that time, in answer to his questions, she had told him about her father and had mentioned her hope of finding her brother in Cheyenne. But the rattle and roar of the stage had made extended conversation impossible. Now he decided that the panic he had noticed earlier must in some way be connected to her search for her brother.

"Is it your brother?" he asked gently.

She straightened up. He brought his arm back. "Yes," she said, a trace of anger in her voice. He saw color rise to her cheeks as she thought of it. "I went to see the man Everett worked for—and he refused to tell me anything. Kyle, I think he knows something. I think he's done something to Everett!"

"Easy, Caroline. Easy. Let's just eat this apple one bite at a time. First of all, what's this gent's name?"

"Brian Wallace."

Kyle frowned. He knew Brian Wallace, had dealt with him more than once on his trips to Cheyenne. The man had always struck him as honest and aboveboard. "Go on," Kyle said.

"He didn't seem to like Everett, and when I told him I was Everett's sister, he got very nervous. Then all he wanted was for me to go back to the ranch and my father. He just wanted to get me out of Cheyenne, Kyle, and he wouldn't tell me anything about Everett. He's hiding something. I'm sure of it."

"Does sound strange at that. If your brother worked for him, there's no reason why he shouldn't tell you where he is. If he knows, that is."

"Oh, I'm sure he knows! Kyle, you must help me. Go with me to see him, please! I'm sure you'll be able to persuade him to tell the truth."

"All right, Caroline," he said. "I'll go with you. But simmer down. I know Brian Wallace. I've had dealings with him in the past, and he always struck me as fair enough. We'll go see him first thing tomorrow and get this straightened out. I'm sure it's just a misunderstanding."

"Oh, Kyle, can't we go see him right now—tonight?"

Kyle shook his head regretfully. "I wish we could, Caroline. But I promised to help the captain and the sheriff. There's a mean crowd gathering outside the jail, bent on lynching that Indian the captain's bringing back to New Mexico. I only came over here to see how Tim Moody and Seth were doing."

At that moment Sarah Crouse reentered the room. Kyle got to his feet. "How's Tim doing, ma'am?" he asked.

"My name's Sarah," she grumped. Then she looked at Caroline. "Now maybe you can introduce me to this here tall drink of water."

Caroline hastily introduced Kyle.

Shaking his hand heartily, she looked up at him and said, "Tim's still unconscious, but he looks a mite better. There's some color in his cheeks, and he seems to be sleeping quieter than before. And Seth's all right, too. He's upstairs in the back bedroom, snoring so loud he's making the shingles rattle." She smiled then. "I must say, he sure appreciates a woman's cooking. The doctor took care of his wound in no time. The only thing was, he'd lost so much blood."

Satisfied, Kyle moved toward the door. "Guess I'd better get back to that jail, then," he said to Caroline.

Caroline nodded and accompanied him from the room. Kyle was reaching for the knob to the front door when Seth, looking somewhat shaky, came down the stairs. He waved weakly and managed a grin when he saw Kyle.

"How do you feel, Seth?" Kyle asked.

"Weak as a kitten, but outside of that, I'm fine."

"Good," said Kyle. "Where you headed now?"

"Thought I'd look in on Tim, then mosey on down to the express office. See what I can do to help out. They ought to be sending out fresh horses to Devil's Creek pretty soon."

"Reckon so," said Kyle. "But I wouldn't push myself too hard, if I were you."

Seth pulled up shakily at the foot of the stairs. "Don't worry," he said. "I couldn't, even if I wanted to."

"Now listen here, Seth," Sarah Crouse said. "Before you go anywhere, you get into my kitchen first. There's some hot soup and fresh biscuits out there."

Seth grinned at the woman. "Just as soon as I look in on Tim," he promised, moving on past her.

Kyle opened the door and turned to look at Caroline. "I'll be back as soon as I can tomorrow," he told her, "then we'll go see Wallace. I'm sure he'll help you find your brother. Like I said, it's probably just a misunderstanding. Trust me."

"All right," Caroline said deliberately. "I will."

As Kyle left the boardinghouse and hurried through the streets to the sheriff's office, he wondered if, in making that promise to Caroline, he might not have been a mite too quick. He wanted to help her, sure enough. But that was no excuse for promising what he might not be able to deliver.

He was still pondering this dilemma when he turned a corner a few minutes later and saw the enormous crowd packed into the street in front of the sheriff's office. His heart sank. From the look of things, Santoro was in deep trouble. There was no way Kyle and the others could keep that crowd at bay.

It took Kyle only a second to make his decision. He swiftly turned away from the crowd and hurried down the street toward the livery stable.

A half hour later, the hot breath of the crowd on his back, Kyle Warner was let into the sheriff's office. As Sheriff Bounty quickly closed the door behind him, Kyle looked around the room and saw Captain Farnum standing by the window, a rifle in his hands. He was regarding Kyle with a sardonic smile on his face.

"Thought you might have changed your mind, Warner," he said.

"Maybe I should've," Kyle replied. "That's some mob out there. They act like they've been feeding on raw meat for a week."

Without much conviction, the sheriff said, "We'll hold 'em."

Kyle saw the town constable, a double-barreled shotgun in one hand, peering unhappily out at the street through a side window. The man was all skin and bones, with a long neck and frightened eyes. His Adam's apple bobbed almost continuously as he watched the crowd. Huddled in the corner were two desperate-looking townsmen, both of them armed with shotguns as well. They looked very unhappy indeed. These, Kyle realized, must be the citizens the sheriff had persuaded to act as deputies. They impressed him no more than the town constable did.

"How's the Apache holding out?" Kyle asked.

"Damn!" spat the sheriff. "He's an Indian. He don't feel nothin'."

"He's been quiet enough," the captain responded.

"You mean you ain't checked on him lately?"

"Hell, Warner," said the captain. "There's no need to concern yourself with the Apache. He's secure, don't worry."

"You mind if I check?"

"Go ahead," said the sheriff, exasperated. "Then get back out here. This crowd is getting ready to try something. I can feel it in my bones."

"I can *hear* it," Kyle said, as he pushed open the door to the cellblock and entered it.

He approached Santoro's cell without saying a word.

Santoro was standing up, both hands clasping the bars. They still were manacled. The Indian saw him approaching but made no outward sign that he recognized Kyle. For a moment Kyle wondered if the sheriff might be correct in thinking that the Apache felt nothing.

Not daring to say anything until he had checked out the cellblock, Kyle continued on past Santoro, inspecting the four other cells. He was immediately glad he had. A drunk was sleeping it off in a cell in the corner. The swelling tumult from the growing crowd in front caused the man to stir fitfully.

"Hey!" Kyle called in to the fellow. "Hey! You ready to get out of here?"

The man blinked with comical suddenness and sat up on the bunk, scratching his unruly hair. Focusing his eyes with some difficulty, he picked out Kyle standing just outside his cell and cleared his throat. "Hey, what in hell's goin' on out there?"

"A lynching. You want in?"

The man snatched his battered Stetson up off the floor and scrambled to his feet. "No, dammit to hell! I don't!"

Kyle returned to the sheriff's office.

"I think we better let that rummy out of the corner cell," he told the sheriff. "No sense in him getting mixed up in this."

"Terry Shad still in there?" the sheriff exclaimed. "Hell, I'd forgotten all about him!"

Kyle held out his hand. "Throw me the keys. I'll let him out."

The sheriff took a heavy ring of keys down from a hook over his desk and tossed them to Kyle.

"Which key?" Kyle asked as he caught the ring.

"The biggest one fits them all," Bounty said, hurrying back to the window.

Kyle returned to the cellblock and unlocked the door to Shad's cell. As the fellow gratefully stumbled past him out into the sheriff's office, Kyle hurried over to Santoro's cell, unlocked it, then pulled the door open a few inches.

His eyes met Santoro's. The Apache hesitated. Kyle put a finger to his lips, then motioned for Santoro to pull the door shut and wait.

"Trust me," whispered Kyle.

With a barely perceptible nod, the Apache pulled the door shut.

On his way out of the cellblock, Kyle inspected the back door. It was padlocked shut, but a swift kick, he was sure, would break it open. The window beside it, however, was securely barred. As he turned to move back out to the sheriff's office, he found his way blocked by Captain Farnum.

"What the hell's goin' on between you two?" Farnum demanded.

"I don't know what you mean," replied Kyle.

"You don't, huh?" the captain said, striding past Kyle and over to Santoro's cell. He grabbed the door and pulled it open. "What's this supposed to mean?"

Kyle shrugged casually. "No sense keeping the Apache caged with that crowd out there liable to break in here any minute. He deserves better than that."

"Does he now?"

"Yes."

"So you unlocked his cell door, is that it?"

"Yes," Kyle replied emphatically. "That's it."

The captain held out his hand. "Give me those keys," he said.

"I will like hell."

At that moment the sound of shattering glass filled the sheriff's office. Kyle glanced into it and saw a brick lying on the floor and shards of window glass covering most of the sheriff's desk. He and the captain hurried into the room. Glancing out through the broken window, Kyle saw a solid mass of outraged citizens.

A fellow brandishing a revolver cupped one hand around his mouth and shouted in to them, demanding that they get out now and let the crowd take care of the Apache. The crowd roared its approval and began to surge still closer. The fellow with the revolver jumped up onto the wooden sidewalk.

The sheriff straightened his shoulders and strode toward the door. Kyle and Farnum joined him. Bounty hesitated a moment before opening the door and glanced back at the constable. The man had his back flat against the wall, and huddled alongside him were the two terrified deputies. It was obvious that the only thing holding them up was the wall. As Kyle had surmised earlier, there would be no help from that quarter.

Sheriff Bounty turned back around and pulled open the door. The three men strode out to face the mob.

Chapter 7

The first thing the sheriff did was to unceremoniously push the fellow with the revolver off the boardwalk. The man sprawled backward and was caught in the arms of those just behind him. Then the three men formed a line facing the mob. About half-a-dozen men held blazing torches. Their flickering light added a hellish note to the proceedings.

Standing there facing the crowd, his feet wide and his six-gun out, was for Kyle like standing in front of a raging inferno—except that the heat came from hate, not those few flickering torches. He sucked in his breath and did his best to keep his knees from turning to jelly.

Beside him, the sheriff cleared his throat and raised his hand to silence the crowd. It quieted expectantly, as they assumed that the man was willing to make a deal. Kyle's glance flicked from one deranged face to another. He shuddered. The three of them were facing a slavering, hydra-headed beast whose bloodlust was already in full cry.

"Go back to your homes!" Bounty thundered at them. "You've had enough entertainment for one night. This Apache is on his way to New Mexico and an Army trial. Leave it at that!"

"We will like hell!" someone in back shouted.

"Trial, hell!" another man cried out. "We'll give him one right here—at the end of a rope!"

As the crowd surged still closer, Bounty again held up his hand. "I warn you!" he cried. "The first man who tries to get into this jail after that Apache will get a bellyful of buckshot!"

"Stand aside, Sheriff!" a powerful-looking man in the front ranks told Bounty, his voice carrying above the angry murmur of the crowd. "We got no quarrel with you. It's that Apache we want!"

"Bart," the sheriff replied. "You know me. And you know I mean what I say. It don't matter who you think you got this quarrel with. Right now, you got a quarrel with the law. I'm the law in this county—and right now in this town. So back off! I'm warnin' you!"

"No, Sheriff!" someone behind Bart cried out. "*You* back off! We want justice!"

This was the fellow who had been haranguing the crowd most of the evening. At his side, Kyle saw, was the fellow with the rope. Even as the man behind Bart cried out for justice, his companion raised his hangman's rope over his head, turned around, and beckoned the crowd to advance on the sheriff's office.

That did it. As if it were a herd of longhorns stampeding on a moonless night, the mob instantly surged forward. Those in the front ranks were pushed, scrambling up onto the boardwalk. Rather than fire point-blank into them, Bounty whirled and ducked back into his office, Kyle and the captain swiftly following after him.

As the sheriff closed and bolted the door, he glanced at Kyle. "You take one window. The captain can take the other one. I'll watch the door. The first one through it, I'll cut in half."

Kyle didn't believe him. Too many of those men out

there were the sheriff's friends. They were liquored up now—not entirely responsible for what they were doing. Knowing this, there was no way the sheriff was going to cut loose on them.

But Kyle had no love for any of them. Poking his revolver out through the broken window, he sent a few rounds over the heads of those nearest. After all the threats and counter-threats, these few rounds were the first shots fired that night. For an instant the mob scrambled to a halt. A few men started to dive back hastily—until someone answered Kyle's shots with a blast that took out what was left of the window.

As splinters of glass peppered him, Kyle ducked away. Outside, a vicious chorus of shots erupted, followed by the heavy boom of a shotgun. The other window exploded inward, and Kyle could hear the buckshot slam into the wall outside, just under the window. Peering out, he saw at least five men carrying a telegraph pole among them, charging the door. A second later, the ram slammed into the door. The upper panel shattered but held. The men recoiled to try again, as covering fire from the now thoroughly aroused crowd sent rounds humming through the open windows.

Ducking low, Kyle bolted for the cellblock. He nearly tripped over the constable and the two deputies, who by this time were lying flat on the floor, wincing at each round that plowed into the walls above their heads. Before Kyle reached the cellblock, however, Farnum loomed up before him, blocking his way.

"Where you going, Kyle?" he demanded. "We need you out here—not in there with that Apache!"

"Don't try to stop me," Kyle said. "No one in here's

got the sand to stop that mob. I'm getting Santoro out of here. Now!''

"Dammit! That Apache's my responsibility!''

"Not anymore. Give me the key to his manacles.''

Without thinking, the captain reached up to finger a cord hanging around his neck. With a grim smile, Kyle grabbed the cord and yanked hard, snapping it. The captain struck out at Kyle in an attempt to take back the key, but Kyle roughly shouldered him aside and slipped past him into the cellblock.

At that moment they heard the splintering sound of the battering ram as it broke through the door. Kyle glanced back into the sheriff's office in time to see the head of the telegraph pole hastily being withdrawn. A second later, boots began kicking at what was left of the door. As it began to sag inward, a growing crescendo of roars from the crowd outside punctuated each slam of a boot.

The captain glanced back at Kyle. "All right," he said. "Do what you have to do! I'll cover you!''

With a quick nod, Kyle hurried over to Santoro's cell and pulled open the door. Santoro strode out, a smile flickering momentarily over his dark face.

"This way, Santoro," Kyle said, heading for the rear door.

As they reached it, the door to the sheriff's office gave way and the crowd stormed in. Kyle heard the sheriff cut loose with both barrels. There were screams and oaths, followed by the ragged rattle of pistol and rifle fire. Glancing over his shoulder, Kyle saw two bloodied townsmen staggering back into the arms of their comrades, while the sheriff buckled and sagged to his knees.

Kyle turned back around and kicked the rear door just above the knob. The nails holding the padlock gave way, but the door held. A second kick slammed the door open wide, and the two dashed out into the night.

As Kyle ducked through the doorway, he glanced back in time to see the captain going down under the furious onslaught of a storm of irate citizens.

"This way!" Kyle told Santoro. "Over here."

Running ahead of Santoro along the darkened alley, Kyle came to the two horses he had tied up to a rear-porch railing. Untying their mounts, both men swung into the saddle. Glancing back toward the chorus of shouts behind him, Kyle saw the crowd spilling furiously out into the alley after them. Shots were fired. Kyle didn't bother to return the fire as he clapped spurs to his horse's flanks and galloped along the alley for a couple of blocks, then turned his mount back onto the nearly deserted main street and headed out of town. A very disorganized and mightily frustrated crowd cursed fruitlessly in their wake.

As dawn broke over the badlands north of Cheyenne, Kyle and Santoro pulled their lathered horses to a halt and wearily dismounted. They were off the trail, deep in the bowels of a canyon, a towering wall of rock at their back, a shallow stream trickling past them. Kyle's intention was to sleep during the day and travel by night, at least while they were still in Wyoming Territory.

Santoro was no longer wearing the manacles Captain Farnum had had fashioned for him. Once they were clear of Cheyenne, they had pulled up to let Kyle unlock them. It was during this pause in their flight that Kyle had explained to Santoro his plan to let the Apache live with him on his horse ranch as a full partner. He had explained eagerly to the impassive Indian that his ranch in Montana was so isolated that there was no doubt Santoro would be well out of reach of the Army or any prying officials of the

Bureau of Indian Affairs. The Apache had listened without comment, then nodded and stepped back up into his saddle.

Now, too weary to say much, the two men unsaddled their horses and let them loose, their legs hobbled, on a grassy sward on the other side of the stream. Opening his sugan, Kyle nodded wearily to Santoro and went to sleep, his head pillowed on his saddle, his back against the cool flank of the canyon wall—and his right hand closed firmly around the grips of his Colt.

He was awakened by a vague sense of unease.

Sitting up, he saw that Santoro's bedroll was gone— as were the Apache and his horse. Glancing up at the sun, he saw that it was not too much higher than it had been when he had closed his eyes. Scrambling to his feet, he pulled on his boots and rolled up his sugan. Not long after, he found the Apache's tracks. To his dismay, he saw that Santoro was making a wide circle to the south.

It was noon when Kyle glimpsed the Apache topping a rise in the distance, better than four miles ahead of him. For a moment the tiny figure shimmered in the heat haze, then vanished. Kyle drove his horse to its limit, and by midafternoon Santoro was in sight. Kyle raised his six-gun and sent a round into the air. Santoro pulled up, and Kyle waved. Santoro turned his horse into a nearby patch of timber and dismounted to wait for Kyle to reach him.

When Kyle finally rode up to him, Santoro was sitting cross-legged on a floor of pine needles, his back to the trunk of a tree. He watched impassively as Kyle wearily swung out of his saddle and took off his hat to beat the dust off it. Slapping it back on, Kyle took a deep breath and approached the Indian. He was angry. But more than that, he was puzzled.

"How come you ran off like that, Santoro?" he asked, squatting down in front of the Apache.

"I do not wish to go north and work with the horses on your farm. I am an Apache. I am not a White Eyes."

Kyle nodded. He could understand that—at least some of it. "Sure, you're an Apache, Santoro. Nothing can change that. I wasn't aiming to do anything of the kind. The thing is, on my ranch you'd have freedom to come and go as you wanted. And you could save money. You'd be a full partner. After a while, you could buy your own ranch. You'd make a great breeder."

"I am an Apache, not a breeder of horses."

"It wouldn't make you any less an Apache if you bred horses. I've seen you with horses—you and your people. You're good with them. The best. And once you've got property and money, the government can't touch you."

The Apache smiled. "The White Eyes will find a way. I am an Apache. They will either kill me or shut me on a reservation. You are crazy to think you can change anything. So now I go back to my people. It was foolish for me to seek the aid of the Sioux. They are fools. They think they can stop the White Eyes without help, and they refuse to forget old quarrels with the Apache. So my dream is over."

"Is that why you came up here? To seek an alliance with the Sioux?"

"Yes. Only one Sioux chief agreed with me. Crazy Horse. But in the councils of his tribe, he is shouted down by old women."

Kyle took a big breath. *Jesus*, he thought. *Thank God for those old women*. If Santoro had succeeded in uniting the western tribes against the white man, with the Apache and Sioux leading the alliance, it would have spelled disaster for the West—and for ranchers like himself.

Kyle stood up. "Santoro," he said. "When you left the reservation, were you alone?"

"No. Four young warriors go with me. I chose them myself. They had much anger and were eager to show they were true Apache."

"Did you go through a settler's place nearby?"

"Yes."

Kyle was afraid to ask the next question, but he forced himself. "Did you take anything from that settler, Santoro?"

Santoro glanced up at Kyle for a long moment before replying. Then he looked away, his hooded eyes brooding. "Yes," he said.

"I'd like you to tell me about it, Santoro."

Without looking back at Kyle, Santoro told him what had happened. At first the settler and his wife had seemed perfectly willing to sell them the horses and provisions they needed. But while the Apache were selecting their horses, the settler and his wife came up on them from behind with loaded shotguns, with the intention of capturing them and alerting the Army.

It was a simple matter for the Indians to distract and disarm the man and his wife. And that was all Santoro had intended to do. But that was not enough for the younger Apache. They killed the settler and his wife—and their children—as painfully as they could, as a punishment for their treachery, then rode out. So displeased was Santoro with their behavior that as soon as they were clear of the territory, he told them to leave him and go their own way, insisting that he would travel north to the land of the Sioux without them. And so he had.

When Santoro finished his account, Kyle slumped

back against a tree. He had defended Santoro in his discussion with the captain, and now here was Santoro confirming in most particulars the captain's charges. Still, Kyle had been partially correct. Santoro himself, if he could believe the old Apache, had not instigated the murders. Furthermore, the Indians *had* been provoked. Nevertheless, no matter how you cooked or seasoned it, a military court would most assuredly assign the blame to Santoro. Kyle stepped away from the tree.

"I won't try to convince you to go north with me if you don't want to, Santoro. But where are you going now?"

"I go to join Victorio."

Kyle nodded. He wasn't surprised that Santoro would choose to join the chief who once had united the Chiricahua Apache and led them in raids against their white enemy. "This is good-bye, then," Kyle said.

Santoro got to his feet. "You have saved me from the many White Eyes—and from the captain—just as Santoro saved you and your family. Now we owe each other nothing more, Kyle Warner."

Kyle nodded and stuck out his hand. The old Apache took it and shook it. The old Indian's grip was powerful. For a moment his black eyes regarded Kyle with something approaching affection. He turned abruptly, swung into his saddle, and, with a wave, rode off.

Kyle watched him go for a while longer. Then, with a sigh, he mounted up and swung his horse to the southeast—in the direction of Cheyenne. He had some explaining to do to the captain, and a promise to keep—a promise he had made to Caroline Wells.

Chapter 8

Later that same day, the Donner brothers, riding bare-back and using torn strips of Flem's shirt for reins, pulled their horses to a halt on the crest of a pine-studded ridge and dismounted. Below them was the Devil's Creek way station.

Luke was considerably leaner than he had been when he had first set out from Fort Laramie to rob the stage—so lean, in fact, that his receding chin seemed to have vanished altogether. Beside him, Flem too had lost much of his bulk. He now had a wan, shrunken look. Folds of dirty, unshaven skin hung from his cheeks, giving him the appearance of an oversized bulldog. So filthy and disreputable did the brothers look that they might have aroused hilarious laughter if they had been on a music-hall stage, peering out at an audience and nudging each other while they scratched at their flea-bitten hides.

But any hilarity their appearance might have generated would have vanished soon enough, once members of the audience caught the insane gleam in both men's eyes.

Leaving their horses, they slipped cautiously down the slope toward the rear of the log building, then pulled up in a patch of alders and studied the situation carefully. Despite their hunger, they were in no hurry as they watched the way station below, with the patience of wild animals who know their unsuspecting prey soon will be twitching between their jaws.

A man in a black suit, whom they recognized as the gambler, Dirk Taggart, left the station and walked across the yard to the barn the Sioux had left standing. As Luke watched the gambler disappear into the barn, he felt his mouth water. A thin, wolfish smile flickered on his narrow features as he glanced at his brother.

"Look at that, will you?" he said. "That sonofabitch is still there."

"I hope his woman is, too," Flem whispered.

Even as Flem spoke, Louise Thompson appeared in the yard. She was carrying a bucket of dirty water. While they watched, she dumped the bucket of water onto the ground, then proceeded over to the well. They heard the squeal of the pulley as she lowered the bucket.

"Don't see anyone else," said Flem. "The station-master should still be in there. And his wife. We got a score to settle with that bitch, too."

"We will," said Luke softly. "We will."

They waited until both the gambler and his woman had returned to the station house before leaving the trees and continuing on down the slope. There was a woodlot in the timber behind the building. On top of a newly stacked cord of wood, Flem found an ax, its blade imbedded in an uncut log. He worked the blade loose, then hefted the ax.

Grinning at his brother, he said softly, "I got what I need right here."

"Let me have your Bowie," Luke said.

"Get your own weapon," his brother snarled.

Luke had expected that response. He knew how much his brother favored his Bowie. Quickly glancing around, he saw what appeared to be a small crowbar resting under a split log. He pulled it free. It was a wrecking bar the stationmaster must have used to pry apart the logs he was splitting. Luke hefted the wrecking bar, then looked over at Flem.

"Keep your damn knife," he whispered softly. "This here'll do just fine."

"How we gonna work this?" Flem asked.

"I'll come in the front door. That should catch their attention. Then you come in the back door with that there ax." Luke's eyes danced with anticipation. "It shouldn't take long."

Flem moistened his thumb and ran it lightly along the blade of the ax. "Hell," he said. "It won't take long at all."

It was still broad daylight, in the middle of the afternoon, with a bright, almost blinding sun beating down on them. Yet they appeared to be cloaked in a kind of darkness as they moved openly toward the way station. They could hear the low hum of conversation coming from within the building as Flem flattened himself against the wall beside the back door. Luke left him there as he turned the corner of the building and walked almost casually up onto the low porch and kicked open the front door.

As the door swung wide, Luke glimpsed the station-master standing by the kitchen stove, holding a cup of coffee, his wife beside him with a coffeepot in her hand. Closer to the door, Luke saw the gambler rise from a table and start to turn, his right hand dropping to the Smith & Wesson on his hip. Luke swiftly jumped into the room and brought his wrecking bar down. But the gambler's woman materialized from his right and pushed Taggart away. The bar struck both her and the gambler. Luke felt it smash across the side of her head, then glance onto the skull of the gambler. Both of them crumpled to the floor before him.

That was when Flem burst in through the door behind

the stove. The stationmaster's wife screamed. Her husband tried to fling her to one side, but Flem's ax caught him solidly in the chest and cleaved him neatly. He seemed to disintegrate in a sudden fountain of red. The woman screamed again as Flem raised his ax a second time, then she collapsed in a faint before him. Flem swung at her halfheartedly, catching her on the side of the head. She was flung over by the force of the blow, her large torso jerking spasmodically as her opened skull spilled a bloody gruel over the floor.

Flem swiftly stepped over the two bodies, his bared upper torso drenched in blood. "Jesus," he said softly. "That's the last time I'll use an ax! That Bowie of mine is a hell of a lot neater."

Luke grinned at his brother. "You look like hell. Check the bedroom for a clean shirt. I'll scare up some grub."

Heading for the bedroom, Flem said, "Make it quick. I'm hungry enough to eat the bark off a tree."

Luke found a sack of wrinkled apples in a cupboard under the sink, then a loaf of freshly made bread in the bread box. He was ripping into the loaf with his teeth when he found the salt pork and beans in a kettle on the back of the stove. It was cold and needed to be reheated, but he snatched up a wooden spoon and began shoveling it into his mouth without bothering to heat it.

His brother was soon beside him, his upper torso now covered by one of the dead stationmaster's red-checked cotton shirts. Snorting and elbowing each other aside like famished animals at a trough, the two soon made short work of the salt pork and beans. But they still were not content, and were searching the cupboards for more food when they heard the rumble of a stagecoach as it pulled into the yard.

"Hell!" cried Luke as he looked out the window. "Here's our transportation to Cheyenne. Finish up. I'll go talk to the driver."

"Don't let the sonofabitch in here," Flem said, wolfing down the rest of the bread.

Luke didn't bother to answer as he ducked out the door and pulled it shut behind him. The stage was already rumbling to a halt, the horses fighting their bits as the Jehu hauled back on the reins. Luke strode over to the stage and peered up at the driver.

"I need fresh horses!" the driver called down to him impatiently.

"There ain't none," Luke replied. "Ain't you heard what happened?"

"I heard about the Sioux attack, sure," the driver replied, releasing the brake. "So has everyone else. It sure has discouraged passengers. Thing is, I was hoping they might've sent out fresh horseflesh from Cheyenne by this time."

"They ain't sent nothin'."

The driver looked beyond Luke at the door of the station building. It was sagging slightly inward on its hinges. "How's Ty Wilks and Miranda? They all right?"

"Hell, no, they ain't all right. Them Sioux weren't very polite when they came for them horses. Seems like horses wasn't all they came after. They took a few scalps back with them, too."

A round-faced, apple-cheeked tenderfoot, wearing a derby hat, had poked his head out the coach's side window and was listening to all this with wide, frightened eyes. Luke glanced at the man when he told the stage driver about the scalps. For a moment Luke thought the fellow in the derby was going to get sick all over the side of the coach.

116

The stage driver frowned. "Hell, I heard Ty and Miranda had come through it all right."

"You callin' me a liar, mister?"

"It ain't that. It's what I heard. . . ."

"You want to go in there and see for yourself? You're welcome to, if you want." Luke chuckled coldly. "If you've got the stomach for it, I guess you'll be all right."

"Forget it, mister," the driver said quickly. "I'll take your word for it. Anyhow, could be the Sioux came back to finish the job."

"That's right. So if I were you, I'd get a move on, fresh horses or not. I spotted some Sioux on that ridge yonder a spell ago. Looks like them heathen don't much like this here stage line."

"Sioux?" the driver exclaimed nervously. "How long ago was that?"

"Less'n two hours ago."

"Then I guess I'll do just as you suggest, mister," the driver said, reaching for his whip.

"Hold it," said Luke. "Wait for my partner. We're goin' along, too. With the stationmaster and his wife dead, there ain't nothin' further we can do here."

"Hurry it up, then," said the driver, glancing around anxiously.

Luke went back into the station house. Flem was still bent over the stove, scraping the last of the beans and salt pork from the kettle. He had relieved the gambler of his gun belt. The grips of Dirk Taggart's Smith & Wesson gleamed incongruously against Flem's filthy, sunbaked Levi's.

"Let's go," Luke called to his brother. "We got transportation to Cheyenne. And I got a hunch we'll find that double-crossin' sonofabitch there too—all fat and sassy and ready to pluck."

"That sure as hell would be nice," said Flem as he started across the room.

"You finish off those two?" his older brother asked, pointing at the unmoving forms of Dirk and Louise.

"Hell, nothin' *to* finish. You busted open their skulls."

"Good. Let's get a move on," Luke replied, leading his brother out of the building.

Climbing into the stagecoach behind his brother, Luke glanced up at the box. The driver, his whip in his hand, was leaning over to see him into the coach. "Let's get the hell out of here," Luke told the man. "Them Sioux like to attack around sundown, I hear."

At once the driver sent his whip uncoiling out over the backs of his horses. The stagecoach suddenly lurched forward. A grin on his face, Luke quickly slumped back into the seat next to his brother. There were just two other passengers in the coach, both of them sitting directly across from the two brothers.

One was a shriveled old-timer huddled in a corner of the coach, watching them with all the animation of a dead man. Beside him sat the fellow in the derby hat. One look and Luke knew he was a whiskey drummer. He held his leathern sample case on his lap, both arms folded protectively over it.

As the stage rumbled out of the yard, Luke said to the drummer, "Maybe you'd let us have a little of that there liquid nourishment, friend. Whiskey's something we could sure use about now."

"Oh, I couldn't do that," the chubby little fellow asserted anxiously. "These are samples."

"That's what we aim to do," said Flem, drawing his Smith & Wesson and aiming it almost casually at the drummer's nose. "Sample it."

Hastily—so hastily that he almost dropped his case—

the drummer opened it up and passed a bottle across to Luke. The old-timer in the corner didn't stir. He watched through drooping eyelids as the two brothers passed the bottle back and forth between them for a while, then the old man closed his weary eyes and went to sleep.

Captain Farnum was lying on a dirty cot in a room behind the barbershop, which also served as the town's morgue as well as one of its busiest funeral parlors. He had a huge welt under his right eye, and a clean white bandage had been wrapped around his head. He waved carefully when Kyle appeared beside his bed, then pushed himself to a sitting position.

Kyle had learned, as he rode in early that morning, that the sheriff had already been buried, along with the two citizens the sheriff had cut down. The sheepish citizens of Cheyenne hadn't even glanced up as Kyle dismounted in front of the sheriff's office. The deaths of three people, one of them a well-liked and respected law officer, had taken the starch out of the townspeople, and when Kyle had inquired of the captain's whereabouts, he had been told where to find the man in soft, almost apologetic tones.

"You all right?" Kyle asked the captain.

"Sure. It's just a bump, the doctor assures me. Hell," the captain added, smiling through his obvious pain. "I could have told him that, myself."

"You feel like moving?"

"Nope. Think I'll just rest up here for a while. Every time I try to stand up, the world turns into a merry-go-round—without any music or brass ring." He squinted up at Kyle. "You had that getaway all planned, didn't you?"

"You mean those horses I had waiting?"

"That's what I mean."

Kyle nodded.

119

"Sonofabitch," Farnum said quietly, appraising Kyle with a chill nod of admiration. "Ain't you the swift one."

"Like I said, Farnum, there was no way you could have stopped that mob."

"So then the Apache became your responsibility. Is that it?"

Kyle nodded.

"Where is he now?"

"On his way south to join Victorio."

"Good. Our paths will cross again. This time I'll nail him." He looked shrewdly at Kyle. "You want to tell me now what this is all about? You didn't just happen along like that. You were after Santoro from the beginning. Lying here, I've had plenty of time to think, and I remember now seeing you in Fort Laramie, just before I got into the stage with the Apache."

"You got the time for a long story?"

"I got nothing else right now. And you owe me an explanation, I figure."

Kyle pulled a straight-backed chair over to the cot, sat down on it, and proceeded to tell Farnum why he had come after Santoro. When he had finished, Farnum seemed relieved that he had finally heard Kyle's story.

"How did you know," the captain asked, "that I had tracked Santoro into Sioux territory?"

Kyle laughed. "It was all over the northern plains— how you had ridden into Crazy Horse's camp and taken Santoro prisoner. You think something like that is going to go unsung—especially among the Sioux? How did you manage such a feat, anyway?"

"There was no trick in it. The Sioux have no love for the Apache."

"Even so..."

The captain shrugged.

"There's one more thing," Kyle said, as he stood up and set the chair to one side.

"What's that?"

"Santoro told me what happened at the settler's place."

"And?"

"You were right. Partly. Santoro's band killed the settler and his family. But it wasn't Santoro's idea."

"Maybe not. But he was in charge of them braves, so I still hold him responsible." The captain closed his eyes and lay back carefully. "We'll talk about it later, Warner. Right now there's a gang of Chinamen dynamiting a tunnel through my head. Why don't you come back later?"

"I'll do that," said Kyle, tugging his hat down securely. "If you need anything, holler. I'll be at the Crouse boardinghouse."

"Thanks," the captain murmured.

Kyle turned and left.

Caroline felt very much alone—worse, deserted. She had counted so much on Kyle's promise to go with her to see Brian Wallace, and now he was gone. It was not very clear to her what had happened. Some said the Apache had escaped with Kyle, but others protested that Kyle had only tried to prevent them from hanging the Indian.

But whatever the truth was, one fact alone remained—and for her this was all that mattered. Kyle had left Cheyenne. He would not be at her side when she returned to Brian Wallace, as she must, to demand that he reveal her brother's whereabouts. Abruptly, she put down her needlepoint—her heart simply was not in it—got restlessly to her feet, and went to the window to look down at the crowded street.

She just couldn't get Kyle out of her mind. Images of

the tall, enigmatic man had filled her since he had first loomed against the rocks back at the Devil's Creek way station, a smoking rifle in his hand. He had saved her life, but what she felt for Kyle Warner was much more than simple gratitude. To her growing exasperation, she had been finding it increasingly difficult to look into his eyes without blushing. And whenever Kyle spoke, his voice sent shivers up her spine.

She did not entirely like what all this implied. To be this much in the thrall of another human was almost frightening. Perhaps, she told herself with grim irony, it was better that he had left. Now she was free of him. She would no longer find herself acting like a love-struck schoolgirl whenever that tall galoot appeared before her. But if that was so, why did this knowledge fill her with such an aching sense of loss?

She heard footsteps approaching her door, followed by a soft knock. She left the window and pulled open the door to find Kyle Warner standing in the doorway, an apologetic smile on his face.

So stunned was Caroline that she could only stand there, wide-eyed. "Kyle!" she managed finally. "Kyle Warner!"

"That's right," said Kyle somewhat sheepishly. "It's me, all right. Not a ghost."

Kyle, his hat in his hand, stepped into the room. Caroline closed the door behind him, then leaned her back against it, still gazing at her tall, buckskin-clad visitor in some wonderment.

"Is it really you, Kyle?" she asked. "I heard you had run off . . . with that Apache!"

"You heard right. I helped Santoro escape, and I'm not sorry. That mob would have torn him to pieces. I'll tell you all about it sometime, but if I'm not mistaken, I promised to go see Brian Wallace with you. So here I am.''

"Oh, Kyle! And here I was sitting up in this room, certain I would never see you again.''

"No need to worry about that," Kyle told her. "You know what they say about bad pennies.''

"How soon can we go?'' she asked eagerly.

"Right now, if you want.''

Without another word, Caroline plucked her shawl off the back of the chair, flung it over her shoulders, and led the way to the door.

At about the same time that Caroline and Kyle were leaving Sarah Crouse's boardinghouse, Seth Loman was stomping into the Wells Fargo express office. As he closed the door behind him, he turned and found himself staring in some astonishment at two quite outlandish-looking characters who were on their way out of the office. But when Tillman, the manager, saw Seth, he called out to the two men.

"Hold up there, boys," Tillman told them. "Before you get going, I want you to meet that shotgun guard who outfought the Sioux at Devil's Creek. Lum, Wendell— meet Seth Loman.''

The two men brightened at once and advanced on Seth, hands extended.

"I'm Lum Sutter," the tall, rangy fellow announced, shaking Seth's hand eagerly. "It sure is a pleasure to meet a real, genuine Indian fighter.''

"That goes for me, too," said his companion, pumping Seth's hand in turn. "I'm Wendell Lope.''

Seth stepped away slightly, somewhat taken aback by their grinning enthusiasm and their appearance.

Lum Sutter was dressed, dude fashion, in what looked

like a brand-new buckskin outfit, which he had topped with a flat-crowned plainsman's hat. The hat and the buckskin suit nearly shone, they were so clean. It was obvious the outfit had just come out of a box that Sutter had carried with him from the East. The plainsman had an eager look about him, his blue eyes wide and innocent. He couldn't be much more than twenty years old, and he struck Seth as the typical eastern pilgrim, fresh off the train and eager to fight the redskins. And he came loaded for bear—two gleaming, ivory-handled six-guns were strapped to his waist.

His companion was a study in contrast. He had an eagerness to match Sutter's, but it was a feral, beady-eyed eagerness that reminded Seth of a wolf's eyes peering out of the darkness. In addition, Wendell Lope was fat and slovenly, an unshaven hulk dressed in filthy Levi's and a torn cotton shirt. His long, graying hair hung in greasy tails from under the brim of his black, floppy-brimmed hat. Like his companion, he was packing an arsenal capable of starting another Mexican revolution—two six-guns and a shotgun, with a Bowie knife stuck in his belt.

"Lum and Wendell here are going to bring them fresh horses and supplies to the Devil's Creek way station, Seth," Tillman explained. "They'll be leaving this afternoon, soon's we get their wagons loaded up. And we got a nice string of fresh horses to go with them."

Looking away from the two, Seth said, "Hell, Mr. Tillman. I was hoping you'd send me. That's why I stopped in."

"Now, Seth," Tillman said, adjusting his steel-rimmed glasses farther back on his long, delicate nose. "You've done enough for Wells Fargo this month, I'd say. Let these two take them supplies and horses out. They've offered to do it, and for a most reasonable price, I might add."

"You just let us handle them Sioux, Mr. Loman," said Lum eagerly. "We been hoping for a chance like this. Them damned aborigines ain't gonna mess with Wells Fargo. Not with me and Wendell around, that is."

"Them pesky savages are just our meat, Seth," his partner added.

Seth sighed. "You two sound like you been readin' too many of them dime novels Beadle puts out."

"Well, I ain't ashamed of that," protested Lum. "Most everybody back East is, too. Mighty interesting readin'. Shows what a white man has to do to make the West safe for decent men and their womenfolk."

"I ain't read none of them books," said Wendell roughly. "But that don't matter. I don't need to read to know how to handle a redskin. They's heathen, sure enough. One white man's worth ten of them."

"That so?" commented Seth, amused.

"Okay, you two," said Tillman quickly, sensing Seth's growing impatience. "On your way now. And good luck!"

"Don't worry about us, Mr. Tillman," said Lum, tapping his six-guns. "All the luck we need is right here."

Seth watched the two disappear out the door, then turned to Tillman. "Where the hell did you find them two?"

Tillman grinned and shrugged. "They just walked in. Heard I was looking for two men to take supplies out to Devil's Creek. They offered to do it for nothing, but I insisted on paying them."

"Not much, I'll bet."

Tillman shrugged. "Wells Fargo will be pleased, I'm sure, at how little it cost to hire them two *fearless* Indian fighters." He chuckled as he said it.

"Call them back, Mr. Tillman. I won't charge any

more than them. I'm getting all tightened up sitting around this here town.''

"Now listen, Seth. You were hurt pretty bad, lost a lot of blood. We don't want to risk losing a good driver— now that Moody won't be available for a while. So you just rest up awhile longer. There ain't no harm in that.''

"You know I was thinking of quitting Wells Fargo and going with the railroad. You treat me like this and I just might.''

Tillman looked shrewdly at Seth. "I know you were thinking of it. But I know you better than that, Seth.'' Tillman grinned. "And so does Tim Moody.''

Seth found himself grinning back at the man.

"By the way, how's Tim gettin' on?''

"Eatin' like a horse. The doc says he's out of danger— but not really. Sarah's got him all roped and hog-tied, as far as I can see.''

Tillman laughed and started for his desk and the pile of correspondence that cluttered it. "Give him my best, Seth. And Sarah, too.''

"I wish you'd reconsider, Mr. Tillman,'' Seth said. "Those two men might do more harm than good.''

"You mean they're liable to shoot off their toes when they draw their six-guns?'' Tillman laughed. "Forget it, Seth. I'm using them. You take it easy for now. Get your strength back.''

With a sigh, Seth said good-bye and left the office. Once outside, he looked around to see if he could catch a glimpse of those two heavily armed Indian fighters. But he saw no sign of them. With a resigned shrug, he started down the street on his way back to the Crouse boardinghouse.

At that same moment, a few blocks away, Caroline and Kyle were approaching Brian Wallace's freight ware-

126

house. Kyle led the way up the wooden steps to the office and held the door open for her.

The clerk whom Caroline had spoken to on her earlier visit was perched atop his stool, his green-visored head still bent over the piles of invoices and bills of lading on his desk. She let Kyle ask for Brian Wallace, and once again found herself moving through the warehouse past the crates and boxes of machinery and other goods to Wallace's glassed-in office.

Kyle did not hesitate as he knocked on the door, pushed it open, and swept in, Caroline by his side. She thought she detected a sudden look of resignation on Wallace's face the moment he saw her with Kyle.

The two men shook hands cordially. Wallace nodded courteously to Caroline and offered her a chair.

"No, thank you," she told him. "I would rather stand. I don't expect this will take long."

With an audible sigh, Wallace turned to Kyle. "I can guess why you're here, Kyle," he said. "It's about Miss Wells's brother."

"That's the long and the short of it, Brian. Miss Wells has come a long way to find him, and she sure would appreciate any help you might be able to give her." He paused for a moment, then smiled gently. "And so would I."

Wallace slumped down into his seat, picked up a pencil, and scrawled something on a piece of paper. Slapping down his pencil, he handed the paper up to Kyle. "You'll find Everett Wells at this address, most likely. If he ain't there now, he'll turn up sooner or later."

"You see!" Caroline exclaimed to Kyle. "I told you! This man knew all along!"

"Well now," replied Kyle quickly, "maybe so, but

there's no call to beat that horse anymore. Brian's given us what we want, Caroline. Let's go.''

As Kyle opened the door for Caroline, he turned back to Wallace. "Thanks, Brian," he said. "See you around."

Brian Wallace, leaning back in his swivel chair, peered thoughtfully back at them without bothering to respond. Caroline thought he seemed relieved—as if an unpleasant duty was no longer his to perform.

To Caroline's growing dismay, she found that the address Wallace had given Kyle was taking them constantly deeper into the Chinese quarter. She found herself moving closer to Kyle as they picked their way down noisome alleys and narrow streets, past disreputable shacks and buildings—all the while surrounded by a swarm of Orientals who parted before Kyle's tall striding figure like waves before the prow of a ship, their high-pitched, singsong chatter filling the air like a frightening, alien chant.

At last Kyle pulled up in front of a two-story building that appeared to have lost not only its front door but most of its upstairs windows as well. He looked down at Caroline and passed her the address Brian Wallace had given him.

"Here we are," he said grimly. "This is the place."

Caroline read the address. Then she looked back up at the house and shuddered.

"You ready, Caroline?" Kyle asked gently.

"Couldn't there be some mistake, Kyle? Maybe Brian Wallace just gave you this address to get rid of me."

"That's a possibility," he admitted. "But we'll never know for sure standing here."

"I guess you're right," she said. She handed back the address and took a deep breath.

Kyle led the way into the building. Following on his

heels, Caroline almost tripped over a sleeping form huddled in the hall just inside the doorway. They proceeded a few feet down the hallway before Kyle pulled up abruptly. A large, burly Chinese man was effectively blocking their way.

"I want to see your head man," Kyle told the man crisply. "Where is he?"

"You wait here," the big fellow replied. "He'll come soon."

"I'll wait."

The man turned and shambled swiftly down the dim hallway, disappearing into a doorway at its end. Caroline heard the sudden jabber of raised voices—all in a Chinese dialect—and a moment later, an incredibly ancient Oriental stepped into the corridor and moved swiftly through the gloom toward them, his clasped hands out of sight within his long, drooping sleeves.

On his wizened face she saw a thin straggle of white chin whiskers as wispy and insubstantial, she felt, as the spirit that must dwell within such a frail creature. He was dressed in gleaming black silk pants and jacket, the seams of which were ornately trimmed with red brocade. On his head he wore a black, conical hat.

Behind him, Caroline saw two taller, much less frail Chinese. They did not look at all friendly.

As the old man came to a halt before them, Kyle nodded politely. At once, the ancient Chinese returned Kyle's nod, then turned his face slightly to acknowledge Caroline's presence as well.

"Welcome to the humble abode of the unworthy Li Chan," the frail phantom of a man said to Kyle, his voice as thin as a reed, but surprisingly clear. "That your Excellency's heaven-born splendor would waste his time on so mean a hovel as this fills this humble servant with wonder and appreciation. Would you allow the least of your slaves to inquire as to what great wind of good fortune has brought you here?''

Kyle seemed momentarily taken aback by the man's overblown speech. But he recovered his composure quickly. "This here 'heaven-born splendor' is visiting this mean hovel in the company of Caroline Wells," he told the old man. "She's searching for her brother, Everett Wells. We were told he might be here—or would soon show up.''

Li Chan turned then to look more closely at Caroline. For just a moment Caroline thought she caught a flicker of concern, perhaps even compassion, in Li Chan's eyes.

Abruptly, the old man looked back at Kyle. "If your splendid personage would please to follow this unworthy guide.''

Kyle looked at Caroline. "Guess that means he'll take us to your brother, Caroline.''

Li Chan bowed. "If this is what your Excellency wishes. But the miss, perhaps it would be best for her to wait here?''

"No," Caroline told Li Chan firmly. "I'm going, too.''

Li Chan bowed slightly to Caroline, then turned and led the way down the dim hallway.

As Caroline followed with Kyle, she could not help noticing that the two larger Chinese—bodyguards, she had no doubt—were padding along right behind them, moving as swiftly and as silently as Li Chan. Their soft yet powerful tread so close upon her gave Caroline an uneasy feeling. Indeed, by this time her heart was filled with misgivings.

What on earth was Everett doing in a place like this?

Suddenly they plunged down a steep, twisting stairway. The darkness was Stygian. She could see nothing.

And all she could hear was the faint rustle of the old man's silken pants just below them on the stairs. She tried to keep as close as possible to Kyle without treading on his heels. Foul-smelling, guttering candles finally appeared below them. They were set on narrow beams and gave the only light as they continued circling down to a level Caroline was sure must be well below street level.

At last they came to the bottom of the stairs. A narrow passageway, shored up by rough timbers, yawned before them, with a tiny, flickering pinpoint of light over a door at the far end of it. As they moved on down this passageway, Caroline heard the scuttering of tiny feet in the darkness.

Rats!

She shuddered and moved still closer to Kyle. He took her hand in his, squeezing it tightly. That helped a little—but only a little.

As they approached the door, Caroline saw another heavily built man standing with folded arms in the shadows beside it, as silent and impassive as a Buddha statue. When they reached the door, the guard stepped out of the shadows and pulled it open for them. Li Chan ducked his head and entered, Kyle and Caroline following in after him.

Caroline saw they were in a long, narrow corridor with another door at the far end. Fish-oil lamps cast a dim yellow glow over the place, and the dirt floor was puddled in spots from the water that seeped through the ceilings and darkened the overhead beams. Kyle, she saw, was barely able to stand upright as he followed Li Chan through the passage.

Shivering in the dampness, Caroline felt a pall of apprehension fall over her. An alien, incomprehensible evil seemed to dwell in this subterranean world. She couldn't imagine what her brother could possibly be doing in such a place—but whatever it was, it couldn't be good.

When they reached the end of the passage, there was another door, with still another huge Chinaman guarding it. Li Chan said something in Cantonese to the guard, and the door was immediately opened for them. They followed Li Chan through it and found themselves in a long room, or den. The air was fetid. A sweet, cloying odor engulfed them. Caroline felt her senses begin to reel.

"Kyle," she whispered. "What's that smell?"

"Opium smoke," Kyle replied somewhat grimly.

Opium smoke! Caroline felt herself shrivel inside. Kyle's words evoked a depraved, heathen underworld inhabited by wretches caught in the clutches of a habit so vile, so destructive, that for all intents and purposes their very souls were lost to them. Could Everett possibly be mixed up in a traffic so cruel—so heartless? The thought caused the blood in her veins to run cold.

As they moved on into the den, the thick coils of smoke shifted heavily in the dim candlelight. The walls on both sides of them were fitted with bunks, six tiers high, with very little space between them. Each bunk held a man who was either in the act of doping up his opium pipe or was already deeply asleep, wrapped in blissful dreams.

And the dreamers, Caroline was shocked to see, were not Orientals but white men!

Li Chan stopped at the far end of the den and pointed to a figure in one of the bunks. As Caroline stopped before Li Chan and looked into the bunk, she let out a tiny cry of horror.

The smoker was asleep, his long, emaciated fingers closed over his precious pipe, his lean face cadaverous, his ribs clearly delineated in the dim light. The only clothing he wore were threadbare cotton pants and a filthy pair of stockings.

Caroline had found her brother.

Chapter 9

Mary Beth Smith hurried through the streets of Cheyenne. She had decided at last that she could no longer deny her love for her son—or his need for her. No matter how difficult it would be for her, she was determined to go back to her husband. She owed it to Caleb. Only a truly wicked woman would leave her son with a man like Amos.

Now, her heart thudding in her breast, Mary Beth entered the lobby of the Cheyenne Rest and approached the desk clerk. After a quick perusal of the register, the clerk confirmed that her husband was registered, and he directed a young bellhop to escort her to Amos's room on the second floor. After the bellhop left her in the dim hallway, she turned to the door, took a deep breath, and knocked.

She heard the harsh, guttural snarl of her husband somewhere in the room, then the squeak of bedsprings. His heavy, angry tread approached the door. Mary Beth braced herself as the door was flung wide.

The look on Amos's face upon seeing Mary Beth was a mixture of fury and triumph. "So!" he cried. "It's you, is it!"

Mary Beth stood trembling in the doorway, her eyes searching for her son, who turned from where he had been standing at the window. He cried out and hurried toward his mother. Brushing past her husband, Mary Beth entered the room and embraced young Caleb.

Amos pushed the door shut behind her and watched them. The look of triumph he had exhibited a moment before gave way now to a dark, glowering expression. He took a deep breath and strode toward the two of them.

"Is it true, then, woman?" he demanded. "Have you come to your senses at last?"

"Yes," she told him boldly. It was surprising, but now that she had her arms around her son, her debilitating fear of this man seemed to have evaporated. "I'll return to the farm with you—but you must never lay a hand on me again."

"What's this, woman? You telling me what to do? How I should chastise my own wife?"

"Yes, I am. You want me to cook and clean for you? I'll do that, and I'll help you bring up our son. But in return, you may no longer chastise me, as you call it. I am done with that, Amos. You lay a hand on me again, and you'll find me gone—this time for good."

Amos pulled himself up to his full height. Mary Beth saw once again the confused, shaken coward she had witnessed on the doorstep of Sarah Crouse's rooming house when that woman had refused him entry. Amos was a bully, she realized, and like all bullies simply had to have his bluff called. Almost giddy now in the warmth of her son's embrace, she was calling her husband's bluff.

Amos laughed. It was an ugly, shattering sound. His sharp, barking laughter congealed the blood in her veins. Again she felt the awesome, numbing terror he was capable of arousing in her.

In that instant all Mary Beth's hard-won confidence vanished. For too long Amos had enjoyed complete domination over her. It was no longer possible for him to relate in any other way. For him to dominate her with ruthless terror was more than habit now—it was an immutable part of his nature.

Abruptly, Amos's cruel laughter ceased as he reached out and yanked Caleb free of Mary Beth. Caleb spun sickeningly and crashed into the wall, then slumped to the floor. As he stirred groggily and tried to get back up onto his feet, Mary Beth saw the tears of rage coursing down his cheeks.

That was when Amos struck her.

The blow caught her on the side of the head. For a moment she remembered nothing until she struck the floor behind her. Blinking her eyes frantically so that she could see where Amos was, she found him towering over her, laughing again. He reached down, grabbed her by the hair, and yanked her brutally to her feet.

"Now, Mary Beth. Tell me that again. About how you ain't gonna let me chastise you no more. Go on. Let me hear that!"

"It's true!" she cried, through her tears. "I won't."

"Yes, you will!" Amos said, slapping her with such force that the right side of her face went numb.

Bright shards of color exploded before her eyes. She found herself gasping for breath. In a mindless excess of rage, Amos shoved her back sharply against the wall. The back of Mary Beth's head struck it with such force that she blacked out momentarily. When she could see again, she was on the floor a second time, and Amos was standing over her once more, arms akimbo, laughing.

"Now," he said, "let's hear it again. You didn't get it right the first time. Are you gonna let your lord and master chastise you?"

Mary Beth knew she should agree with him—say anything that would placate him at this moment. But somehow she couldn't get herself to do it. He might beat her into insensibility, yet still she would not give in. These past few days of freedom from him had made it impossible for her ever again to bow meekly before his cruelty.

Doggedly, aware of the blood now trickling down her chin, Mary Beth shook her head. "No," she managed. "Never!"

"Damn you to hell!" Amos cried, hauling back and kicking her in the side with terrible force.

Gasping in pain, Mary Beth rolled over. Again, she had difficulty catching her breath. Through pain-slitted eyelids, she saw Amos approaching her once more. He was beside himself, releasing now all of the pent-up fury he had been storing since she had first run away. He was no longer in control of his emotions, and in that instant, she became certain he was going to kill her—as she had once seen him beat a dog to death with his rifle butt because it had refused to come to him when he had called it to heel.

But a sudden, piercing shout caused Amos to hold up and spin around. Mary Beth glanced over and saw Caleb standing before the bed, his father's enormous Colt revolver in his hand. He held it out in front of him with both hands, and its muzzle did not waver as he trained it on Amos's chest.

"You leave Ma alone!" Caleb cried, tears streaming down his cheeks, his eyes wild with grief.

"Now you put that gun down, boy!" Caleb's father commanded.

"No, I won't!"

"You hear me, boy? I'll whup you good and proper if you don't put that down!"

Caleb flexed his knees and raised the gun an inch or so. Mary Beth saw his hands tighten around the weapon.

His face became hard with resolve. "You go ahead and whip me," the boy said bitterly. "You just see how much good it'll do. But you won't never kick Ma again! I won't let you! If you do, I'll kill you."

Amos moistened his lips nervously. "Now, see here, Caleb. There ain't no need for you to threaten your own father."

"Yes, there is!" Caleb cried. "There ain't no other way to get you to stop! Now, you get away from Ma! Stand back!"

Amos stepped away from Mary Beth. "Okay, son. I done just like you told me." He stuck out his hand and started toward Caleb. "Now you just give me that gun before it goes off and hurts someone."

Caleb took a quick step back. "Stop right there, Pa! Don't you come no closer."

"Dammit, boy!" Amos said, in a sudden fury of exasperation. "I done what you said! I stepped away from your ma! Now you give me that gun!"

"No, Pa! I don't trust you. I'm taking Ma out of here with me so you can't never hit her again!"

"No, you ain't," Amos blustered. He started resolutely toward his son. "You ain't doin' nothin' of the sort. Now I'm gonna take that gun from you and give you a lesson you won't soon forget!"

In a panic, Caleb stumbled backward, lowered the six-gun, and fired. The detonation filled the hotel room with a shuddering thunderclap as the round slammed into the floor at Amos's feet. Astounded, Amos held up at once, his face suddenly as gray as old newspaper.

He looked down at the hole at his feet, then glanced up with abject fear at his son. "Now, lookee here, son," he cried, his voice quavering. "You got to put down that gun. *Please*. I promise—I won't try to take it from you!"

Compressing his lips, Caleb lifted the gun and steadied it; the sound of its hammer cocking shook the small room. "Next time," Caleb said through gritted teeth, "I'll shoot higher! Right in the gut, Pa! Now you step back there, over by the window!"

Amos hesitated. "Son, you can't do this! I'm your—"

"You heard me, Pa!" Caleb said, cutting Amos short. "Get over by that window."

Amos gave up then. He slouched over to the window. As he moved, Caleb tracked him with the revolver.

"All right, Ma," the boy said, his eyes still on his father. "Let's get out of here!"

Mary Beth didn't hesitate. Scrambling to her feet, she rushed at the door and pulled it open. Caleb, with the enormous revolver still trained on his father, followed her out the door. As Mary Beth pulled the door shut, Caleb stuck the gun into his belt, then hurried down the corridor alongside his mother.

They had reached the landing when Amos flung the door open behind them. "Caleb!" the man cried. "Come back! You can't leave me alone like this! I'm your pa!"

Amos cried out again, but his cry of rage and despair didn't deter his wife or his son as they continued on down the stairs and out of the hotel.

Everett Wells lay in a stupor on Caroline's bed in Mrs. Crouse's rooming house. When Kyle had first plucked the frail dreamer out of his filthy, smoke-filled bunk and slung him over his back, he had been appalled at how light the man was. Later, when he had dropped Everett onto Caroline's bed after the journey through town past curious and astonished citizens, Kyle stood back to peer down at the still-sleeping man and found, to his surprise, that he was barely winded. He might as well have been carrying an oversized sparrow.

Caroline had gone ahead for a doctor, convinced that something more terrible than opium had eaten away her brother's once robust physique. When Dr. Miles—the same doctor who had tended to Seth and Tim Moody—entered the room with the distraught Caroline and saw Everett's pitiable condition, he pulled up at the foot of the bed and shook his head. Then he opened his black bag, took out his stethoscope, and began to examine the emaciated dreamer.

When the doctor finished his examination, however, he looked at Caroline and Kyle with a bemused expression. "Heartbeat steady, if a touch feeble . . . pulse normal," he said, shaking his head slightly in wonder. "Aside from a severe case of malnutrition, Mr. Wells is still well enough physically to survive, I'd say. This young man has a tough disposition, and that's a fact. There's no other way to explain how he's managed to last as long as he has. I've come across this fellow before." He took off his glasses and began to wipe them as he looked back down at Everett. "Whatever he has eatin' at him, it sure as hell is hanging on something fierce."

"I don't understand, Doctor," Caroline said. "Will Everett be all right?"

Doc Miles nodded. "If you can keep him out of the Chinese quarter. And away from the saloons."

"I see," Caroline said with a sigh. She knew she would have considerable difficulty following his prescription. "You . . . you said something else, Doctor—something I didn't understand. You said there was something eating at my brother. What did you mean by that?"

The doctor put his steel-rimmed glasses back on and shrugged wearily. "I don't know for sure myself, Miss

Caroline. Just a feeling I have about the way this young man—and others like him—have taken to the pipe. I can't help thinking there's something bad—positively malignant—driving them.''

"Something malignant? You mean . . . the Devil, Doctor?"

"That's what some would call it." He dropped his stethoscope into his bag, then closed it. "But I'm not sure it's that simple."

"Doctor, what can I *do*?"

He gazed at her with evident sympathy. "I told you. Keep him out of the Chinese quarter."

"But . . . suppose he won't let me?"

"Then you must *make* him let you. You have no other alternative, Miss Caroline."

With a curt nod, the doctor moved past Caroline and Kyle and left the room. As the door closed behind him, Caroline looked helplessly at Kyle, who shrugged and looked down at her brother.

"Guess he's right, Caroline. You'll have to keep your brother away from the opium. And meanwhile, I suggest you get some food into him. He doesn't look very healthy to me."

Everett Wells stirred. Caroline hurried to his side and bent close.

"Everett!" she whispered. "Everett, it's Caroline!"

The emaciated form on the bed stirred a second time. Everett looked up at his sister with clouded eyes. Smiling dreamily, he turned his head toward the window.

"Everett?" she whispered again, somewhat more urgently this time.

"It's taking a while for him to come out of it," Kyle said.

Caroline straightened. Everett looked back up at her,

141

the dreamy smile gone from his wasted face. He frowned. Abruptly, he pushed himself upright. "Caroline!" he gasped. "Is—is that you?"

"Of course, Everett."

"What are you doing here?" And then he looked around in sudden panic. "Where am I?"

"Please, Everett," Caroline pleaded. "Lie back down. I've come to take you home. Father needs you. He's sick, very sick."

"You've come—to take me back?"

"Yes, Everett. I told you. Pa's a very sick man." Everett shook his head as if to clear it and snorted contemptuously. "Sick, is he? Who . . . who sent you here? Sure as hell not the old man."

"Of course it was, Everett!"

"I don't believe you." Everett's eyes closed momentarily, as if he was recalling a forgotten dream. "I was never man enough for Pa to stomach. Never had his swagger."

Softly, Caroline said, "Father's not swaggering now, Everett. And he *does* want to see you."

Everett slumped back down in the bed and turned his face away from Caroline. "If he's as sick as you say, we'll meet before long—where it's hot enough to singe both our damned souls. Then we'll talk—no sooner."

Caroline looked with sudden despair at Kyle, then glanced back at her brother. "Please, Everett. Don't talk like that. You'll feel better when you get some food in you."

Everett suddenly looked back at his sister, his sunken eyes blazing. "I don't want food, sis. You know what I want!"

Kyle stepped closer. "You won't be puffing on them pipes anymore, Everett," he said. "And I suggest you get used to the idea. Caroline's come a long way to fetch you, and she's not goin' to be disappointed—if I have anything to say about it.''

"Who the hell are you?"

"A friend."

"I got no friends."

"Maybe not. But your sister does."

Everett glanced at her with sudden, withering contempt. "*Your* friend, is he? What're you giving him in return?"

Caroline blushed, tears suddenly filling her eyes.

Kyle rushed at Everett, then held himself back. "If you weren't such a pitiful specimen, mister . . .''

"Please, Kyle," said Caroline. "Don't. He's . . . he's so sick. He doesn't know what he's saying."

Kyle took a deep breath. "Maybe."

"Perhaps it would be better, Kyle, if you . . ." She didn't have to finish for Kyle to read what her eyes pleaded.

"Sure thing, Caroline," Kyle said, putting on his hat. "Just so you don't let this tinhorn buffalo you none. You can maybe lift him up, but you'll have a hard time keeping him there."

He nodded good-bye to her then and left. He was better than halfway down the stairs when he heard a muffled cry from Caroline's room. He halted and looked back in time to see Everett burst out of the room, a wild look in his eyes. When he saw Kyle on the stairs below him, he pulled up for a moment, then started recklessly down the stairs, his eyes still ablaze.

"Out of my way, mister," he cried, his voice thin with hysteria. "I'm not staying in this place! I got better friends in Chinatown."

But Kyle swung around on the stairs, completely

blocking Everett's progress. In a fury of frustration, the man took a swing at Kyle, who easily warded off the blow. It was as if some oversized insect had flailed at him with one of its weightless limbs. But when the fellow persisted, Kyle lost his patience, grabbed the man's wrists, swung him around, and booted him—ass over teakettle—down the stairs.

Everett came to a halt with a resounding thump at the foot of the stairs. He was beginning to stir sluggishly when Kyle reached him and hauled him to his feet. Everett blinked woozily.

"Can you hear me?" Kyle demanded.

Everett struggled to focus his eyes on Kyle, who began to shake him, roughly. Everett's long, untidy hair flew wildly, and for a moment Kyle was certain he could hear the man's teeth rattling in his head. Everett's eyes flew open and he stared fearfully at Kyle.

"Can you hear me now?" Kyle asked a second time.

Everett managed a nod. "Yeah! Yeah, I hear you!"

"Good!" Kyle said grimly. He stopped shaking the man. "Now you listen and listen carefully. I want you to go back up those stairs to your sister. Right now she's the only friend you got. And you're staying in her room until you get that opium out of your system."

"No," Everett said tightly. "I am not!"

Kyle pushed Everett, then released him. Surprised, Everett rocked back unsteadily on his feet. With careful deliberation, Kyle swung on Everett, his big fist catching the tip of his chin. Kyle didn't lean completely into the punch, since he had no desire to break the man's jaw. Nevertheless, Everett was knocked completely around before he crumpled to the floor.

Kyle heard Caroline cry out in protest, and glanced up the stairs. Caroline was standing in front of her open door, leaning over the balustrade, tears streaming down her face. There was a growing purple welt on her right cheek; obviously her brother had not been gentle with her when he bolted from the room. Even more angry than before, Kyle looked back down at her brother.

Everett was wearily pulling himself to his feet. Once again, his eyes appeared to be fogging over. Reaching out, Kyle grabbed the man's arm and yanked him closer.

"All right, mister," Kyle demanded, his voice laced with fury. "Let's go over that one more time! Where did you say you were going?"

Everett shook his head to clear it, then moistened his dry lips. "Back upstairs," he said hastily. As he spoke, a thin trickle of blood appeared in the corner of his mouth.

"All right, then. Now remember this. If you raise a hand to your sister one more time, I'll finish what I started down here, only I won't be so gentle. Is that clear, friend?"

Everett appeared to slump. He nodded wearily. "Yeah," he said. "It's clear—clear enough."

As Everett turned and started to pull himself slowly back up the stairs, Tim Moody and Mrs. Crouse stepped from the doorway leading to the kitchen. They had witnessed the entire episode.

"You mind telling me what that was all about?" Moody asked. The strapping stage driver's left arm was in a sling, and he looked a mite thinner than he had when Kyle had first seen him perched atop the stage.

Succinctly, Kyle told him about Caroline's brother. When he finished, Tim nodded briskly, left Mrs. Crouse, and started up the stairs after Everett.

"Let's go, young man," he said to Everett. "You ain't goin' nowhere 'til we get you all filled out and dried out."

Then he glanced back downstairs. "Don't worry, Kyle. We'll give this specimen a good bath, a shave, and a haircut, and make sure he stays where he belongs." Then he looked past Everett at Caroline, waiting for them at the head of the stairs. "Won't we, Miss Caroline?"

"Yes," she said hopefully. "That's right, Tim. Thank you."

She took her brother's frail arm and led him toward her room, Moody following after. Kyle watched them go, then snugged his hat down more securely and left the boardinghouse. He felt badly about the way he had treated Caroline's brother, but although it had been distasteful, he realized it had been necessary. The trouble was that he might have turned Caroline Wells against him in the process. This thought was not a welcome one, but he accepted its implications with a fatalistic shrug. After all, if he saw too much more of Caroline, he was going to have to tell her straight out how it was that he had managed to appear on the scene when he first had—and how close he had come to not returning to Cheyenne at all, despite his solemn plea that she trust him to do just that.

Thrusting this unpleasant fact from his thoughts, Kyle strode on down the street, heading for the barbershop where that morning he had left the injured Captain Farnum.

Chapter 10

Earlier that same day, Santoro sat on his horse at the crest of a ridge that afforded an unobstructed view of the Devil's Creek way station. Still on his way south to New Mexico, the Apache had no intention of tarrying, but after a quick glance down at the way station, he pulled up, curious.

The door of the building was hanging open. There was no woodsmoke coming from the chimney. Bird calls, he noticed, were echoing close—too close—to the building. A rangy jackrabbit moved across the yard, paused to peer through the open door, then moved off with careless, unconcerned hops.

The way station had the smell of death about it.

Santoro glanced skyward. No vultures hung in the still air, but that meant nothing. The birds of death only gathered at feasts their eyes found. Santoro knew he should ride on. He wanted to resume his long journey south to his own drier, sunnier land. For too long had he tarried in this chill north country on an errand only a fool could have imagined.

The enmity each tribe held for the tribes surrounding it did not die easily—even now, while their land was being consumed by the White Eyes. The White Eyes thought and fought as one. The Indians refused to do either. Santoro's people—the Apache—were one nation, the Sioux another. And so they would remain, until the White Eyes lopped off each tribe, one by one.

All Santoro wanted now was to return to his people and join Victorio. Perhaps he could convince the chief to unite with Geronimo and rise up once more. To die in battle against the White Eyes was all they had left.

Yet, even as he told himself this, Santoro held his mount steady and continued to study the way station below him. He knew that four people should be in there: the stationmaster, his wife, the Man-With-Death-In-His-Face and the Woman-Who-Pleased-Men. These last two he had liked very much. During the miserable stagecoach ride to this place, they had gladdened Santoro's weary soul with the pleasure they found in each other. He had wished mightily that he had been allowed to drink from the bottle the man had offered him. That these two had so displeased the captain had served only to increase Santoro's appreciation of them. He could see that, like Santoro, they too hated the horse soldiers.

What could have happened to them? Santoro asked himself.

He pulled his horse around and slanted it carefully off the ridge and down onto the meadow fronting the way station. When he splashed across the small creek, there was no hail from within. Santoro's heart grew heavy. All he would find within the log building was death. Of that, he was now certain.

He dismounted a few feet from the open doorway. His horse could smell death now, and snorted as it whisked its tail nervously. Santoro dropped the reins over the hitch rail and entered the building.

The Man-With-Death-In-His-Face and the Woman-Who-Pleased-Men were sprawled on the floor together, just inside the door. They appeared to have been beaten with a gun or rifle barrel. There was an ugly gash on the side of the woman's face, and a bloodied patch of hair on the top of her companion's skull where he had been struck.

Farther into the cabin, beside the stove, were the crumpled, bloody bodies of the stationmaster and his wife. They were both dead, Santoro saw in a single glance. Their end had been terrible, but swift. Anxious to put this place of death behind him, Santoro had started to step back toward the door when he thought he detected a slight, barely perceptible movement in the woman sprawled at his feet.

Bending closer, he rested his ear on her chest. Her heart was beating, but so softly that he couldn't be sure his old ears were hearing correctly. Then he placed an open hand before her mouth. He felt the moisture on his palm and smiled. The-Woman-Who-Pleased-Men still lived. She was sprawled on top of the man, and Santoro had to pull her off to examine her companion more closely. He grunted in surprise to find that he, too, was still breathing.

But they were close to death—so close that even now they were perched precariously on the entrance to the next world. For a moment Santoro wondered if they should be allowed to continue their journey together . . . but only for a moment.

Grunting slightly from the exertion, the old Apache lifted the woman in his arms and carried her into the bedroom, placing her down on the bed. A moment later, he carried in the Man-With-Death-In-His-Face. This one was as light as a bundle of sticks. Once the two were on the bed beside each other, he swiftly undressed them, placed the woman as close to the man as he could get her, wrapped her limp arms around him, and then flung over them what blankets he could find.

If they were going to live, the combined heat of their bodies, trapped under the blankets, would revive them. It was the only medicine Santoro could provide for them now. It would have to do.

Next, he found some bed sheets and wrapped the dead stationmaster and his wife in them, then dragged them from the building and deposited them in the woodlot in the rear, where he could burn the bodies later. Returning to the building, he checked to make sure that the two in the bed were still alive, then went out to scour the hillsides and low places beside the creek for herbs and roots. When he had gathered up what he deemed sufficient, he brought them back to the cabin, built a fire in the wood stove, and made a stew of the herbs and roots, mixing in some salt pork he found. Soon the pungent aroma of the stew filled the cabin.

Santoro left his savory brew to simmer on the stove while he returned to the bedroom and waited hopefully for the two to regain consciousness.

When, after a few more hours, they remained comatose, he found more blankets to heap over them. When this failed to bring them around, he began rubbing their hands between his rough palms, working for more than an hour before being rewarded at last with the first flickering signs of consciousness on the woman's face. Her eyelids fluttered, and then she was staring across her companion's pale shoulder at Santoro—panic, then wonder showing in her face.

"Stay close to your man," Santoro told her. "You give him warmth of your body. Stay quiet. I will bring food."

Santoro brought her a bowl of the soup and patiently spooned it into her. She took as much as she could, then lapsed into a deep sleep. Not long after, the man awakened also. Although his eyes looked closely at Santoro, it was obvious that he didn't recognize the Indian or know where he was. Nevertheless, Santoro managed to spoon-feed a good portion of the stew into him before the barely conscious gambler dropped his head and sank into a profound sleep.

Santoro was pleased. Their hearts were beating more powerfully now, and some color had returned to their faces. He was sure they would live. He left the building, unsaddled his horse, and let it graze in the lush meadows on the other side of the stream.

For the rest of that day, he hovered over his two patients as each returned to consciousness for longer and longer periods. Each time, despite their dazed condition, Santoro spoon-fed them his herb stew. By nightfall, clasped in each other's arms with the piled blankets still covering them, they had both fallen into an untroubled, healing sleep. Exhausted himself by this time, Santoro left the building and found a spot close beside Devil's Creek to make his solitary camp.

What followed for Santoro was the deepest, most refreshing sleep he had enjoyed since the captain had first enclosed his wrists in those hated iron manacles.

Captain Farnum was no longer resting on the cot behind the barbershop, but Kyle found him in Frenchy's Saloon after a brief search, his hat sitting precariously on top of his still-bandaged head. The captain was clutching a stein of beer the way a drowning man would a rope someone had just thrown him. As Kyle sat down, Farnum peered over at him through slitted eyes.

"That beer help any?" Kyle asked.

"Not much," replied the captain. "But since nothing else does either, it sure as hell can't do any harm."

"You don't look so good."

151

"And that's just how I feel. Worse part of it is, I might live."

A bar girl stopped at the table. Kyle told her to bring the captain another beer and a whiskey for himself.

As the girl left, the captain said, "Notice how quiet it is in here? This whole town's got a bad case of the regrets. And a good thing, too. Otherwise, you'd be in real trouble right about now."

Kyle shoved his hat back on his head and looked around. The tables in the back were crowded with poker players, a thick halo of smoke hanging over the green felt tabletops. The clink of poker chips and the sound of kissing dice came clearly to him. The bar was packed solid, and as Kyle glanced along its length, quite a few men quickly looked away as their eyes met his.

Yes, they all knew who he was—and soon enough one of them was going to amble over to give him some trouble. Kyle expected it. In a way, he was looking forward to it. He was not one bit sorry for what he had done, and he would welcome the chance to tangle with any of those bravos who had been responsible for that lynch mob the night before.

"I told most everybody," the captain said, "that the Apache turned the tables on you—that otherwise you would have brought him back as soon as the town cooled off."

"You didn't need to do that," Kyle replied. "But thanks, anyway. You don't think, do you, that anyone really believed it?"

"Of course not. But it gives them an out if they don't have the stomach for any more trouble. And most of them don't."

Their drinks came. Kyle paid the girl and lifted the whiskey to his lips. A shadow fell over their table. Kyle glanced up, then leaned back with a cold smile on his face. The young cowpoke standing over him was swaying slightly, his eyes were red-rimmed, and he was obviously filled to the brim with as much indignation as whiskey.

"Hey there, mister! Ain't you the bastard what let that Apache escape?" he demanded thickly.

The quiet saloon grew even more silent. The sound of rolling dice and clinking poker chips ceased immediately, as everyone held their breath and waited eagerly for Kyle's response.

"Go on back and hold on to that bar," Kyle offered generously. "Come see me when you're sober and I'll be glad to discuss the matter with you."

"Godamighty!" the man cried. "You ain't a-goin' to weasel out of this as easy as that!"

He was a tall fellow with all the heft of a rake, with sky-blue eyes and sandy hair that ran down to his shoulders. He lifted his battered hat and ran his long fingers through his hair, then slapped the hat back on. This action almost caused him to lose his balance, so excited had he become.

"We can settle this right here and now," the young cowpoke insisted, "if you've a mind, you dirty, Indian-lovin' bastard."

Kyle got to his feet slowly, the smile no longer on his face. "That's the second time you called me that, mister. The first time I figured it was a mistake—or maybe the firewater talkin'. But not this time."

The fellow put down his head and charged. Kyle stepped aside and, as the cowpoke swept past, grabbed the man's hat and yanked the brim down over his eyes. Spinning him completely around, Kyle booted the fellow in the rear end, catching him so smartly that he was nearly airborne when he struck the bar. Grabbing hold of it, he clawed himself around and flung his hat to the ground. He was all set to try again.

But before he could get up enough steam, he was restrained by those nearest him and encouraged to cool off. It wasn't that they were trying to protect Kyle. They just didn't want the cowpoke to get hurt.

Turning his back on the young hothead, Kyle sat back down and picked up his drink. The captain regarded him through a painful frown. "You could have made mincemeat of that fellow, Warner," he observed. "That you didn't is to your credit."

Kyle sipped his drink without bothering to respond.

"But of course it was not to your credit that you let Santoro loose to join Victorio."

"That hadn't been my original intention," Kyle replied. "Like I said this morning, I had hoped he would join me at my ranch."

"Surely you must have been prepared for Santoro's reaction. How many Apache have you seen working on horse ranches lately?"

"I guess I wanted it so badly I let my eagerness cloud my reasoning. That might be the explanation, I suppose." Kyle shrugged. "Not that any of it matters now."

"No, I suppose not. But tell me—do you still maintain that Santoro wasn't responsible for what the Apache braves in his party did to that settler and his family?"

"I didn't say that, Captain. I suppose Santoro was responsible—in a way. But you must understand the way these Indians, the Apache especially, respond to authority. Each one is an individual, a law unto himself, bound by no other Indian unless he chooses to be. It's highly unlikely that Santoro would have had any luck trying to restrain those braves."

"Yes, that's quite true. They *are* like that—completely

ungovernable. The West will be a great deal better off when their power to wage war is broken completely. And I intend to do all in my power to bring that moment closer." The captain looked shrewdly at Kyle. "Certainly you can see my point, Warner. Surely you've witnessed yourself the horrors these aborigines are capable of when they go to war—or when they seek simply to redress a grievance."

"I've also seen the horrors white men have visited upon the Apache."

"I'm not prepared to defend any of our own deplorable actions, Warner, but it simply begs the question. The Apache and the white man do not mix. Either we're willing to give this land up to them or we're not. Christian civilization will not allow itself to be held hostage by an insignificant band of heathen. The march of history will see to that."

Kyle was too weary, all of a sudden, to debate the matter any further. There was no way, he realized, that he would ever be able to convince the captain, or anyone else for that matter, that the extermination of a people, heathen or otherwise, was as monstrous a crime as the murder of an individual.

The captain was in the act of reaching for his beer when he stopped and grabbed Kyle's forearm instead. "You know these two?" he asked.

Kyle followed Warner's gaze and saw two men approaching their table. Both men had guns drawn, and the grins on their unshaven faces sent an icy shock of recognition up Kyle's spine.

Yes, he knew Luke and Flem Donner all right.

Clawing for his Colt, Kyle kicked the table over and flung himself out of his chair. He came to rest belly down, his gun up and blazing. His first shots were wild, disintegrating the chandelier over the bar and the mirror behind it. Off to his right, the captain was also firing, but Luke and Flem seemed to have a charmed life as they crouched before them, pouring lead at Kyle and the captain, the thunderous detonations echoing through the rapidly emptying saloon.

Kyle felt his hat fly off and a sharp, stinging sensation in his left shoulder. A round exploded the sawdust in front of his face as he swiftly rolled back behind the overturned table. As lead thunked solidly into it, Kyle poked his head out to the side. Flem Donner was standing up, a wild grin lighting his lunatic face as he continued to fire down at Kyle. Swinging up his Colt, Kyle aimed carefully and fired. This time he caught Flem solidly in the gut. The fellow jackknifed abruptly, an astonished look on his face. As he crumpled to the floor, he squeezed off one more shot, the round taking a large chunk out of the table just beside Kyle's head.

Kyle ducked back behind the table. The captain, his right hand holding his left shoulder, was resting his back against the table, his face twisted in pain.

"Flem!" Luke Donner yelled. "Flem! You hurt bad?" Luke sounded close to panic.

Kyle poked his head up. Luke was bent over his brother, a stricken look on his face. Kyle snapped off a shot that sent Luke's hat flying. Straightening, Luke cocked swiftly and fired back—but his hammer clicked down on an empty chamber. Luke turned then and fled. As he disappeared out the door, Kyle snapped one more shot after him, the slug ripping through the upper section of the batwing doors.

That was the last shot. The abrupt silence came as a blessing. Gradually the ringing in Kyle's ears subsided, but not the thick, acrid clouds of smoke that continued to hang thickly in the air around them.

Wearily, his knees a bit shaky, Kyle got to his feet and helped the captain up. "How's the shoulder?" he asked.

"Went right through." The captain flexed his fingers. "I'm all right, I guess. Hurts like hell is all. At least it takes my mind off this aching head. But what about you?" The captain was looking at Kyle's shoulder.

Kyle reached up. His shoulder wound was sending a thin, warm stream of blood down the front of his jacket. It was only a flesh wound and didn't sting too badly yet, but he knew it would bother him later. Still, after that incredible fusillade, he was lucky to be alive. It could have been a whole hell of a lot worse.

As it obviously had been for Flem Donner.

The saloon's patrons were pouring back into the place now, most of them gathering around Flem's prostrate body. Kyle pushed through the growing ring of onlookers and looked down at Flem. He was gut-shot. Still conscious, his face the color of a bed sheet, a thin trickle of blood seeping from one corner of his mouth, Flem clutched frantically at the hole in his gut. But it didn't do much good. With each gasping breath, his life blood surged through his fingers.

"Someone get him a bottle of whiskey," Kyle said.

A moment later a bottle was thrust into Kyle's hand. Kyle stooped down on one knee beside Flem and handed him the bottle. Flem snatched at it and began to drink greedily. His weapon rested on the floor beside him. It was a gleaming Smith & Wesson that Kyle thought he recognized. Lifting it off the floor, he hefted it thoughtfully.

"Where'd you get this gun, Flem?" he asked.

"That gambler," Flem muttered, pulling the neck of the whiskey bottle out of his mouth. The stench of the raw whiskey was mixing with that of his exposed entrails. "That sonofabitch you left at the way station." His face

157

twisted into a grin. "We killed him and his girl friend."
He took another swig from the bottle. "And Luke'll get
you, too, you sonofabitch. You won't be so lucky next
time."

"What about the stationmaster and his wife? What
did you do to them?" asked Kyle, but Flem's eyes had
already begun to roll into unconsciousness . . . into death.

Kyle stood up and thrust Dirk Taggart's revolver into
his belt. As Doc Miles pushed him aside and knelt beside
the dying man, Kyle made his way back through the crush
of onlookers to rejoin Farnum.

"Who were those two madmen, Warner?" the captain wanted to know. "And why were they after you?"

Kyle hesitated for a moment, considering whether to
tell the full story. But one look at the man's still-bleeding
shoulder and he realized that he owed the captain nothing
less than the truth.

"It has to do with that attempted holdup of your
stage," Kyle said. "These two—and their brother—were
the ones responsible. And I was in it with them. I thought
I could use the confusion of the holdup to free Santoro."

The captain shook his head in disbelief. "You must
have been thinking crazy to attempt such a thing, Warner."

"I guess I can't rightly argue with that. It was crazy,
sure enough. But I figured under the circumstances Santoro's
disappearance from the stage would be chalked up to
Indian-hating highwaymen, so there'd likely be no pursuit."

"And the gold? What did you intend to do with
that?"

"I was planning to take it from the highwaymen and
give it back to Wells Fargo first chance I got. It seemed a
good way to bust up the robbery at the same time I freed
my friend. They would've held up your stage with or
without me."

The captain shook his head a second time.

"I know," said Kyle ruefully. "Like you said, it was a crazy idea. And it went bad the moment Tim Moody squeezed the stagecoach past that boulder. I prevented the Donner brothers from chasing the stage, but it wasn't easy. I had to shoot one of them. Guess maybe I wounded him pretty bad or killed him. Otherwise, he would've been here with his brothers."

"So now what, Warner?"

"I better keep my eyes peeled. Like Flem said, his brother'll try to even this score. But there's something else that worries me even more." Kyle patted the Smith & Wesson in his belt. "Flem had Dirk Taggart's gun. Those two just came from the Devil's Creek way station, and Flem told me he killed Taggart and Louise Thompson." Kyle shook his head in grim frustration. "I liked those two. They didn't have to stay at the way station like that, but they did—and it looks like they paid for that gesture with their lives. But what I'm worried about now is the stationmaster, Ty Wilks, and his wife."

"I can't say as I share your fondness for Taggart and his lady—but I suppose they proved their mettle. Perhaps we should ride out there and check things out. Wilks may be needing help, sure enough, if those two we just tangled with were recent visitors of his."

At that moment Doc Miles left Flem and pushed his way toward them through the growing crowd. The town constable, Kyle noted, still had not shown up. As the doctor pulled up in front of Kyle, he said, "That fellow you shot is dead. Did you know him?"

Kyle nodded. "Name's Flem Donner. He's one of the men who tried to rob the stage."

The little man's eyebrows shot up in surprise. "Looks like his funeral will be on the town, then. I better see to it." Then he frowned with sudden concern at Kyle and the captain. "But first off, you two better let me take a look at those wounds, unless you're both bound and determined to bleed to death."

"All right," said Kyle, "but make it quick, Doc. We got some hard riding to do."

"It won't take long. Get over to my office above the barbershop. I'll join you as soon as I finish up here."

"Let's go," the captain said to Kyle. "That corpse is beginning to stink."

When Kyle and the captain rode out of Cheyenne less than an hour later, they were watched closely by a lone horseman out of sight in the shadows of a water tower.

There was a bloody, makeshift bandage wrapped around Luke Donner's left arm, but it didn't appear to bother him any as he sat astride the big gray he had stolen a short while before from a Cheyenne livery stable. He had had to club into insensibility the old hostler who had caught him in the act.

But Luke wasn't thinking about that now as he urged his mount forward and, keeping well back, followed the two riders out of town and into the growing darkness.

Chapter 11

It was a few hours after dawn of the next day when Wendell Lope and Lum Sutter arrived at Devil's Creek with their wagonload of supplies. Lum pulled the horses to a halt as the two men studied the way station ahead of them.

Behind them, the string of fresh horses moved restlessly on their long tether, the tailboard creaking as the rope sawed against it. Wendell had been told that there were four people staffing the station. Yet, it was well into the morning and there was no sign—absolutely no sign at all—of life about the place.

"I don't like it," said Wendell. "Too quiet. Too damn quiet."

"Yeah," his dandily dressed partner agreed nervously. "It sure is." Lum let his right hand drop to the grip of his six-gun. "Looks like trouble. Right, Wendell?"

"That's what I'm thinkin'."

"You want me to drive up closer?" Lum asked nervously.

"Might as well chance it," Wendell replied. "But keep your eyes peeled." As he spoke, Wendell reached down for his shotgun and planted it across his knees. "Them damn Sioux might be layin' for us inside."

Lum started up the team, an exciting, prickly feeling

161

running up his back as he guided the horses along the rutted road toward the way station.

As they were turning off the main road and into the yard, an Indian in a breechcloth stepped from the only barn that remained standing. He was leading a saddled horse.

"Jesus Christ!" breathed Lum. "Look at that, will you? As bold as you please!" He grinned excitedly at his partner. "I purely *knew* we was headin' for trouble the moment we took this job!"

"Cover me!" Wendell cried, as he snatched up his shotgun and jumped down from the still-moving wagon.

The Apache didn't pause. He left his horse behind and continued to walk toward Wendell.

"Hold it right there, you redskin bastard!" Wendell yelled. "Stand fast, I say!"

Pulling up excitedly and wrapping the reins around the brake handle, Lum jumped down from the wagon, drew his six-gun, and hurried over to back up his companion. The Apache was still walking calmly to meet Wendell.

Wendell drew up in front of the Indian, brandishing his shotgun somewhat wildly. "You just hold it right there!" he cried a second time, obviously close to panic, even though the Apache was apparently unarmed.

The Apache pulled up and stood where he was, seemingly unperturbed as he awaited Wendell's next demand.

"What do you want with me?" the Apache asked. "I have not harmed you."

"What're you doin' here?" Wendell demanded, put off slightly by the Apache's calm tone. "Where is everybody? And where'd you get that horse?"

"It is gift from friend."

"Hah! You expect me to believe that?" Turning to Lum, he said, "Go into the station house. See what's happened to Ty Wilks and his wife—and them other two who was supposed to be here with them."

Lum nodded eagerly and darted toward the building. As he ducked inside, Wendell saw the Apache shift his feet nervously, and took it as a sign of guilt.

Wendell squinted meanly at the Apache. "What's the matter, Injun? Maybe you can feel that noose tightening around your neck already? Is that it?"

A cry came from within the building, and a second later Lum appeared in the doorway. "Wendell! There's a man and a woman in here hurt fearful! And there's blood all over the place!"

"There's just two in there?"

Lum nodded quickly.

Wendell turned to the Apache. "Where's them other two?"

"Behind building. I wrap them in sheets. Both were dead when I come."

"Did you hear that, Lum?" Wendell cried, barely able to contain his excitement. "Go see for yourself!"

Lum disappeared around the corner of the building.

Wendell looked back at the Apache. "You killed them, Apache. Didn't you!" he demanded.

Slowly, the Apache shook his head. "I not kill them. I have no reason to kill them. The woman was kind to me when I was here before. She bring me food. She was not happy to see the shackles on my wrists."

Wendell frowned. "Shackles? . . . You're that murderin' Apache that escaped the jail! Now you've killed two more!"

"I not kill anyone. Ask those inside. They will tell you what happened."

"I'll bet they will! You probably already done tore out their tongues! I read all about you Apache!"

The Apache squared his shoulders fatalistically. "Then do not ask. You would not believe what they say. Believe what you want to believe, White Eyes."

Lum came running. His face was distorted with the horror of what he had just seen. "My God!" he cried, pulling up before Wendell. "Oh, my God, Wendell! I pulled back the blankets and saw them! They'd been mutilated somethin' awful! One was sliced down the middle, and the woman had her head opened up . . . and the flies . . . Lordy! All them flies!" He shuddered and quickly turned away from them, gagging suddenly.

Wendell swung around to face the Indian. "Mutilated!" he cried. "A sure sign of the Apache! It's just like I said, you bloodthirsty heathen!"

The Apache drew his powerful shoulders back, his dark eyes peering with cold contempt into Wendell's. "I tell you truth, White Eyes. You make mistake. I not kill those people."

The Apache turned around and started for his horse.

"Stop right there, Injun!" Wendell cried.

But the Indian, his back ramrod straight, continued toward his horse.

As the Apache reached for the reins, Wendell pulled both triggers. The shotgun kicked powerfully in his hands, and Wendell saw the Apache's body twist grotesquely as the double load of buckshot caught him in the back, cutting him in two.

Kyle and the captain had just spotted the halted wagon in front of the way station when the booming thunder of a shotgun reverberated across the meadowland. At the sound of the shotgun blast, both men, despite the bone-deep weariness they felt after their nightlong ride, spurred their flagging horses to a sudden gallop. Splashing across the stream, they caught sight of two men standing over a dead Indian close to the log building.

With an inward groan, Kyle recognized the horse he had given Santoro, standing just behind the crumpled body on the ground. The two men beside Santoro's body looked up in alarm. As Kyle and the captain bore down on them, the fellow with the shotgun took a nervous step backward. Pulling his mount to a sliding halt, Kyle flung himself from his saddle and advanced angrily on the two men.

"Who the hell are you?" the fat slob with the shotgun demanded.

"Never mind that," snapped Kyle angrily. "Who're you and what have you done here?"

"My name's Lope, and this here's Lum Sutter. What we done is we just killed a bloodthirsty, murderin' Apache, that's what."

The captain swept past Kyle and knelt by the torn body on the ground. After a quick glance, he looked back at Kyle.

"It's Santoro," he said, "near cut in half by that blast."

"That's what I figured," said Kyle tightly. His heart was hammering in his chest. He was glad it was the captain and not he looking down at Santoro's body. A cold fury consumed him as he glared at the two men.

"Why?" he managed. "Why did you kill this Indian?"

The fellow who called himself Lope puffed out his chest and smugly smiled back at Kyle. He was a disreputable-looking sort, in sharp contrast to his companion, a buckskin-clad dude holding a bright, nickel-plated revolver in his hand.

"We caught the bastard in the act!" Lope blustered.

"In the act?" Kyle demanded. "Of what?"

"Of murder!" the dude cried excitedly. "And mutilation! You ought to see what he done! The bodies are out back.''

"I don't believe it," said Kyle. He looked sharply at the dude. "Did you see him kill anyone? You got any witnesses?"

"Sure!" crowed Lope. "There's two survivors inside. If they live, they'll tell you what happened themselves."

"All right," Kyle said. "Let's go on inside and ask them."

Kyle braced himself as he entered the log building, but he was still ill-prepared for what he found. The smell of putrefaction was heavy in the air; and he couldn't miss the bloody discoloration that covered the floor near the stove, nor the shards of scalp and tufts of bloodied hair caught in the bloodstains.

Kyle and the captain had ridden through the night primarily to check on the condition of the stationmaster and his wife, since Flem Donner already admitted that he and his brother had killed Dirk Taggart and Louise Thompson. They were considerably surprised, therefore, to see Taggart sitting up on the edge of the bed, pulling on his britches. Beside him in the bed was a naked Louise Thompson. As the four entered the bedroom, she hastily snatched up a sheet and held it over her fulsome bosom.

One side of her face looked very bad. It was a swollen, purplish mess that completely closed her left eye. The crown of Taggart's frail skull was an ugly-looking tangle of dried blood and hair. It hurt Kyle even to look at it. But both Taggart and Louise were indisputably alive and apparently on the mend.

Taggart managed a crooked smile as he looked up at Kyle. "What kept you?"

"We came as soon as we could," Kyle told him.

"Well, thanks for coming. Now, what was all that shooting out there?"

"This fellow," Kyle said, indicating Lope with a nod of his head, "just got through executing a bloodthirsty, murdering Apache."

Louise Thompson gasped. Taggart swung his death's-head to glare incredulously at Lope. "You did *what*, mister?" he demanded.

"I shot the Apache that done this to you," he blustered hopefully.

"You stupid sonofabitch!" the gambler rasped. "That Apache saved our lives! It was two white men did this to us!"

Louise Thompson began to weep. For a moment, it looked to Kyle as if Taggart was going to hurl himself at Lope. Instead, his face flaming in dismay and anger, he began to cough. Violently. Snatching a handkerchief from his pants pocket, Taggart held it up to his mouth, then sank back onto the bed and rolled over onto his face. The sound of his tearing lungs filled the small bedroom. As he coughed, Louise Thompson forgot the sheet she had been holding up before her and did what she could to comfort the man.

Kyle turned to Lope and Lum Sutter. "Satisfied? You killed an innocent man!"

"Damn!" exploded Lope. "An innocent man! I killed an *Apache*. Who the hell counts them heathen as human?"

Kyle stepped forward and swung on Lope as hard as he could, catching the man flush on the jaw. The force of the blow sent Lope reeling back against the wall. As he slammed against it, Kyle followed after him and punched him again, this time driving his fist wrist-deep into Lope's ample gut. As Lope jackknifed, Kyle brought up his knee, crunching into Lope's nose and snapping his head back sharply. A heavy freshet of blood streaming from his shattered nose, Lope sank, insensible, to the floor.

Kyle spun around then to face the dude. Lum Sutter hastily backed away, flinging up both arms to protect his face. "Don't hit me!" he shrilled. "I wasn't the one shot that Indian! I didn't have no idea Wendell was goin' to do that."

"Unload the wagon and leave those fresh horses," Kyle told the man. "Then get the hell out of here. And take this piece of offal with you. Now, *move!*"

As Lum stumbled hastily from the bedroom, half-dragging his nearly unconscious partner with him, Kyle looked back at Taggart. The man was no longer coughing. Kyle asked him and Louise Thompson to tell them what had happened. When they had finished their account, it was clear that had Santoro not happened along when he did, Taggart and Louise might not have recovered.

Kyle looked at the captain. "Well?"

The captain shook his head sadly. "I guess maybe I owe that Apache an apology, Warner. The trouble is, it's too late now. I truly wish it weren't."

Walking through a pine grove above the valley late that same afternoon, Kyle paused to watch Lope and Sutter pull out. Because of the punishment Kyle had inflicted upon Lope, it had taken the partners all this time to unload the wagon and stable the fresh horses. Meanwhile, Kyle and the captain had been busy with the burial of Ty and Miranda Wilks. Now Kyle was searching for a suitable burial site for Santoro. As the wagon moved off, he resumed his inspection of the pine grove.

It looked out over Devil's Creek and afforded an unobstructed view of the mountains to the west. The prospect was a far cry from Santoro's more arid New

Mexico landscape, but Kyle felt that perhaps here the spirit of his blood brother would rest contentedly.

Satisfied, he started back to the way station.

When he entered it not long after, he found, to his pleased surprise, that Louise Thompson was up and about. Indeed, she seemed already to have transformed the place. Taggart, though still too weak to do anything more than slump back on the cot in the corner of the big room, looked considerably better, also. The stench of death that had seemed to hang over the big room had been banished by the pungent aroma of Santoro's herb stew, which Louise had reheated. She was ladling it out for the captain as Kyle entered, and as soon as Kyle slumped down at the table, she brought him a steaming bowl.

"Find a place?" the captain asked.

Kyle nodded.

"I'll help you—if you don't mind."

"Thanks," Kyle said. "I'd appreciate that."

"I wish I could go with you, too," said Taggart from the cot. "But I don't think I'm up to it."

Kyle glanced over at him. "No sense in overtaxing your strength, Taggart. That was some blow you took."

"Santoro will understand," said Louise softly, as she sat down on the cot beside Taggart.

Kyle finished the soup and stood up. "Might as well get to it," he said.

The captain nodded and got to his feet.

It was close to dusk when Kyle patted the mound of fresh dirt over Santoro's grave with the blade of his shovel and took a small step back. Then, with bowed head, he spoke a silent prayer for the departed spirit of the Apache he had called his brother.

All during his search for this spot and the subsequent

burial, Kyle had been unable to stop himself from wondering if Santoro's death was not his punishment for joining forces with the Donners. By allying himself with such evil in order to free the Apache, had he not invited such retribution? But now, as he stepped back from Santoro's final resting place, he cast this unsettling thought from him and lifted his head. Throwing his shoulders back, he took a deep breath.

What was done was done—it could not be undone. And there was still Luke Donner to contend with when Kyle returned to Cheyenne. Only then, perhaps, would he learn what retribution the fates had in store for him.

"Ready?" the captain asked.

"Ready," responded Kyle.

The two men hefted their shovels and started back through the pines. They hadn't gone far when, from behind them, a voice said, "Hold it right there, gents."

A lean, wasted creature stepped out of the shadows, a six-gun gleaming in his skeletal hand. Luke Donner, it seemed, wasn't in Cheyenne after all.

Chapter 12

The two men spun to face Luke. The man had a bloody bandage wrapped around the upper portion of his left arm, and he favored the arm by resting his left hand inside his belt. But the revolver in his right hand didn't waver an inch, and the mad gleam in his eye burned as fiercely as ever.

Kyle knew he should do something, make some desperate leap to his left or right, even try to rush the man, hoping the surprise of it would enable him to disarm him. But he did nothing. He was too drained by this time.

"Drop your gun belt, you double-crossing sonofabitch," Luke told Kyle. "You, too, Captain."

Kyle unbuckled his gun belt and let it slip to the ground. The captain took his revolver out of its flapped holster and carefully tossed it away.

"It's nice you have shovels," Luke told them. He smiled. "I got a spot all picked out." He waggled his six-gun. "Go on down that trail until you come to the rocks. And move slow. I can just as soon leave you for the buzzards, if you prefer it that way."

Kyle led the way down the trail. Once in the rocks, Luke directed them to a small clearing ringed by boulders. There, Luke told them to begin digging, after which he leaned back against a boulder, covering them.

171

It wasn't until Kyle had nearly finished digging his grave that the anger in him began to percolate through his weary fatalism. Sweat began to pour from him, and he felt his muscles tensing. An almost joyous bravado swept through him. He looked quickly over at the captain. The captain wasn't as far along on his grave, but he glanced up at the same time and caught the look in Kyle's eyes. Kyle thought he saw the captain tensing himself as well.

What the hell! Kyle told himself. *Why should we go meekly, like lambs to the slaughter?*

Luke Donner had delivered himself into their hands. One of them, at least, could reach the man before taking a round. And what did it matter which of them survived to wrap that revolver of Luke's around his skull, so long as the job got done? This animal and his brother had been responsible for the savage murders of the stationmaster and his wife, and indirectly for the death of Santoro.

Besides, it would be fitting if Kyle were to go down with Luke Donner. There would be an ironic justice in that. After all, it was his partnership in that abortive stage holdup that had led, inevitably, to this moment—this final judgment on him.

So be it.

Kyle straightened up, arched his back, then rested a moment on the handle of his spade. The captain did the same. Kyle glanced at Luke. The man had grown alert immediately. He straightened up and stepped away from the boulder toward them.

"You two ain't finished yet," he told them. "Dig it a little deeper. I want to make you sweat. You're both gonna die. You killed my two brothers, and you're gonna pay for that."

"Well, I guess you'll just have to be satisfied with

what I've already dug," Kyle said. As he spoke, he rested the spade on his shoulder and stepped out of the grave.

"Hold it right there!" Luke said. "One more step and I'll fire."

But even as he said this, the captain also stepped out of his unfinished grave and took a step toward Luke. Glancing at both men, Luke moved swiftly to one side so as to be able to train his gun on both of them at the same time.

"You can't get us both, Luke," Kyle told him. "That's a single-action you got there. By the time you cocked for the second shot, you'd be in one of our hands."

"The hell you say!"

Kyle swung his shovel. As the blade cut the air inches from Luke's face, Luke ducked and fired. The spade handle shattered in Kyle's hand. Thumb-cocking instantly, Luke quickly ducked back and leveled his gun at the captain.

"Drop the shovel, Captain," he said, smiling.

Reluctantly, the captain did as he was bid. Holding his stinging hands, Kyle steadied himself, gloomily aware that there might not be any ironic justice after all—just two more murders that Luke Donner would hardly remember in the years ahead.

Calmly, Luke said, "Get on back into that grave, double-crosser. Looks like it's deep enough, so you won't need that shovel, anyway."

But Kyle didn't move. He was still determined to rush Luke. It would be suicide, but at least he would have the pleasure of feeling—if only for a moment—Luke's scrawny neck constricting under his fingers. Tensing, he crouched.

"Go ahead, Warner," Luke laughed eerily, his broken, yellow teeth gleaming in the growing darkness as he aimed his six-gun at Kyle's belly. "Make it easy for me."

As Luke spoke, the frail, ghostly form of Dirk Taggart materialized out of the shadows behind him. The gambler was hobbling along at a painfully slow pace, the Smith & Wesson that Kyle had returned to him held in his right hand. With a quick thrust, Taggart dug the barrel of his revolver into Luke's back.

"Freeze right there, you murdering bastard," Taggart growled, his voice cutting like a knife. "And drop that gun."

Instead, Luke tried to spin away. Taggart fired—twice— each .44 slug catching Luke chest-high. The force of the two rounds flung him back brutally. Kyle stepped to one side as Donner tripped, his gun dropping from his hand, then stumbled into the grave that Kyle had been forced to dig for himself.

It didn't take long for them to bury Luke Donner.

Stepping back from the fourth grave that Kyle had labored over this day, he glanced at Taggart. The man was sitting with his back to the boulder, a handkerchief held up to his mouth. He was no longer coughing.

"Thanks, Taggart," he said.

"Yes," said the captain. "It seems we owe you our lives, Dirk."

"Sorry it took so long to get here. Louise saw the varmint prowling around the building and then watched him follow after you. It took me twice as long to cover the distance as it should have." He grinned up at Kyle. "Looks like I didn't get here any too soon."

"You got here soon enough." Kyle responded.

"Now if you gents would just help me back to that cabin, I think I'd like some more of that brew the Apache concocted, followed by a shot of whiskey, perhaps."

Kyle stepped closer and pulled the frail man gently to his feet. "And we'll both join you," he said.

"With great pleasure," the captain seconded, as the three moved off through the gathering darkness.

The train was about to pull out. The conductors were climbing up into the coaches. The engineer let loose a blast on his whistle, causing a few tardy passengers to hurry across the platform to board the impatient train.

Captain Farnum tipped his hat to Caroline, then shook Kyle's hand.

"I better be boarding," he said. "Keep your powder dry. That's still pretty much Sioux country up there, don't forget."

"I'll remember," replied Kyle.

"Good luck to you, then." He glanced at Caroline. "Both of you."

Caroline felt herself blush. "Thank you, Captain," she said, wishing the man hadn't included her like that.

After all, nothing had really been settled for sure between her and Kyle, even if she and her brother *were* sharing his wagon on their trip back to Montana Territory.

Mary Beth and Caleb stepped forward then to bid the captain good-bye, as did Tim Moody and Sarah Crouse. When they had finished, the captain stood back and saluted them all quite smartly. Then he strode swiftly across the platform, swung up onto the train, and with one final wave was gone.

As the train pulled out, Kyle and Caroline led the rest of them to the street where Kyle had left the small covered wagon he had purchased. Everett had been left with the wagon and was now waiting for them up on the driver's seat, the reins in his hands. He was eager, it seemed, to begin the long journey north that would reunite him with his father.

Everett was now a much sturdier version of the

cadaverous young man Kyle had tossed so easily over his shoulder less than two weeks before. And to Caroline's great relief, he and Kyle had long since buried the hatchet. Indeed, it was Everett himself who had approached Kyle and extended his hand in friendship to the man, thanking him for, as he said, knocking some sense into his head. Now, with each day, it seemed, Everett got stronger and more alert.

Even more important, that unsettling wanderlust that had made Everett such a restless, discontented young man appeared to have finally lost its grip on him, and Caroline was almost ready to believe that he was at last rid of that horrid craving that had threatened to tear him apart before her very eyes.

When they reached the wagon, Mary Beth turned to Caroline. "Well," she said, "now it's our turn to say good-bye to you."

"I'll miss you," said Caroline, hugging the woman. "I hope we meet again."

Caleb, every inch a gentleman, shook Caroline's hand, then blushed violently when she impulsively leaned forward and bussed him on the cheek.

"Next time you're in Cheyenne," Sarah Crouse said, "stop in. If I don't have a room, we can visit. More than likely, Mary Beth will still be with me. I'd be a fool to let go of a woman who can work as hard as she can." As she said this, she squeezed Mary Beth affectionately.

"You'll find me there, as well, Miss Caroline," said Tim Moody, shyly extending his big ham of a hand to Caroline.

As she shook Moody's hand, Caroline smiled and said, "Take care of yourself, Tim." Then she turned to Sarah. "Or maybe I should tell *you* to see to that, Sarah."

"Don't worry," Tim laughed. "She's already done

that. Look at me! Apple dumplings for supper. I'll be as big as a horse before long!''

"Go on! You're just skin and bones still," Sarah protested, laughing.

Kyle cut into the badinage then, shaking Tim's hand heartily, then climbing up onto the seat.

"Kyle," Tim said, "you be sure to give our regards to Taggart and Miss Louise on your way past Devil's Creek. They're goin' to get mighty lonesome out there, but you tell them they're welcome to come in here and stay whenever cabin fever hits."

"I'll do that," Kyle replied.

"I think Louise Thompson is right," said Mary Beth emphatically. "That good air out there and the hard work might be just the thing to pull that fellow through."

"Well, it's a cinch drinkin' and gamblin' wasn't doing that consumption of his any good," said Tim. "Course, that don't mean healthy fellers like Kyle and me have to worry."

They all laughed at that, while Sarah gave the big ex-stage driver a playful jab in the ribs.

Everett stepped over the seat into the wagon as Kyle reached down and helped Caroline up onto the seat beside him. As she settled beside Kyle, she could hardly believe it—they would soon be on their way! She had already wired her father that she had found Everett, and a telegram from him had arrived a few days ago. From its tone she knew how pleased her father was at the prospect of Everett's return—and how grateful he was to her for making it possible.

Kyle, Everett, and Caroline said their last good-byes, waved one final time, and a moment later the wagon was taking them briskly out of town. As they passed beyond the last buildings and set their team onto the rutted road that led north, Caroline found herself thinking once again of Ted Smithers, the rancher who would be waiting for her when she arrived home with Everett.

She would have to give Ted her answer when she returned. And now, at last, she knew for certain what that answer would be: No. It was as simple as that. She had found someone else who did for her what Ted could never do, a fine, sensitive man she would be proud to walk beside for the rest of her life.

Kyle had told her a few days ago of his involvement in the attempted stage holdup and of his reason for doing so, which explained how he had managed to show up when he had at the way station. It sorely troubled him, she could tell, that in stooping to such a deed he had unwittingly inflicted the murderous wrath of the Donner brothers on innocent people. Although Caroline had done her best to comfort Kyle and convince him that she understood and sympathized with the torment he now felt, he was a proud man, too proud to be comforted easily.

Indeed, he still appeared troubled and preoccupied as he sat beside her now, his strong hands holding the reins, his solid chin square and uncompromising. But she knew that a man of his strength of character would eventually come to a just and satisfactory resolution of his dilemma—and that he would find the strength and will to go on from there, wiser than before.

Quickly glancing at him, she wondered how she would ever be able to keep up with such a man. He would always make big tracks. She could tell that from what he had already told her about his ranch deep in the Absaroka Range, southwest of Billings.

And then she remembered that, although she couldn't possibly imagine spending her life with any other man, Kyle Warner had not as yet said anything to her about marriage. Although he obviously cared for her, it seemed to be the farthest thing from his mind.

But then, what did she expect? Kyle was, at the moment, wrestling with some pretty fierce demons. Impulsively, she reached out and took his hand. Kyle quickly looked over at her and smiled, the blush on his face telling her in that instant all she really needed to know. He hadn't asked her yet, but he would. There would be plenty of time between Cheyenne and Billings for her to see to that.

Abruptly, a shout from behind caused them both to turn. At once Kyle guided his wagon off the road to allow a troop of cavalry to surge past them. They were the troopers sent to make sure that there would be no more attacks on the stage line by the Sioux.

As the cavalry clattered past, their bits and spurs jingling as the sun glinted off their saber hilts and rifles, Everett poked his head out of the wagon. "They're Seventh Cavalry!" he told them. "That means Custer!"

Kyle started up the wagon and nodded. "Trouble is, Custer has a habit of taking too much of the bit in his teeth. Wants to do it all himself. Could get him into trouble." He glanced ruefully at Caroline, then took her hand and squeezed it gently. "I should know, after all."

She laughed, then pointed to an approaching stage on its way into Cheyenne. Kyle pulled over once more to let the stagecoach rattle on past them. As it did so, its driver leaned far out from the box and waved.

"It's Seth!" Caroline cried excitedly as she stood up to return the wave. "He's going to stick with Wells Fargo!"

"For now, at least," Kyle said, guiding his team back onto the road. "After that recommendation Tim gave him, I don't see how he could do anything else. And besides,

Seth's got a good hand for horses. It'd be a shame to waste that talent.''

Craning her head, Caroline watched the stage disappear in the distance, a rooster tail of dust billowing behind it. Then she turned back around and sighed, thinking of all that had happened to her—and to those she had come to love—since she had first climbed into that Wells Fargo coach in Billings.

"I hope that sigh means you're happy," Kyle said gently.

"Yes, Kyle," she replied, smiling at him. "I am."

Caroline wasn't exaggerating. She was happy—deeply happy. Not only because she had found her brother and was bringing him back home with her, but because of what she had found out about herself—and *for* herself—during what she would remember for the rest of her days as that truly eventful stagecoach ride to Cheyenne.

**FROM THE PRODUCER OF WAGONS WEST
AND THE KENT FAMILY CHRONICLES—
A SWEEPING SAGA OF WAR AND HEROISM
AT THE BIRTH OF A NATION.**

THE WHITE INDIAN SERIES

Filled with the glory and adventure of the colonization of America, here is the thrilling saga of the new frontier's boldest hero and his family. Renno, born to white parents but raised by Seneca Indians, becomes a leader in both worlds. THE WHITE INDIAN SERIES chronicles the adventures of Renno, his son Ja-gonh, and his grandson Ghonkaba, from the colonies to Canada, from the South to the turbulent West. Through their struggles to tame a savage continent and their encounters with the powerful men and passionate women in the early battles for America, we witness the events that shaped our future and forged our great heritage.

☐	24650	White Indian #1	$3.95
☐	25020	The Renegade #2	$3.95
☐	24751	War Chief #3	$3.95
☐	24476	The Sachem#4	$3.95
☐	25154	Renno #5	$3.95
☐	25039	Tomahawk #6	$3.95
☐	23022	War Cry #7	$3.50
☐	25202	Ambush #8	$3.95
☐	23986	Seneca #9	$3.95
☐	24492	Cherokee #10	$3.95

Prices and availability subject to change without notice.

★ WAGONS WEST ★

A series of unforgettable books that trace the lives of a dauntless band of pioneering men, women, and children as they brave the hazards of an untamed land in their trek across America. This legendary caravan of people forge a new link in the wilderness. They are Americans from the North and the South, alongside immigrants, Blacks, and Indians, who wage fierce daily battles for survival on this uncompromising journey—each to their private destinies as they fulfill their greatest dreams.

TALES OF BOLD ADVENTURE AND PASSIONATE ROMANCE FROM THE PRODUCER OF WAGONS WEST

A SAGA OF THE SOUTHWEST
by Leigh Franklin James

The American Southwest in the early 19th century, a turbulent land ravaged by fortune seekers and marked by the legacy of European aristocracy, is the setting for this series of thrilling and memorable novels. You will meet a group of bold, headstrong people who come to carve a lasting place in the untamed wilderness.

☐	25099	Hawk and the Dove #1	$3.95
☐	23171	Wings of the Hawk #2	$3.50
☐	20096	Revenge of the Hawk #3	$3.25
☐	22578	Flight of The Hawk #4	$3.50
☐	23482	Night of The Hawk #5	$3.50
☐	24361	Cry of The Hawk #6	$3.50
☐	24659	Quest of The Hawk #7	$3.95

Prices and availability subject to change without notice.

SPECIAL
MONEY SAVING
OFFER

Now you can have an up-to-date listing of Bantam's hundreds of titles plus take advantage of our unique and exciting bonus book offer. A special offer which gives you the opportunity to purchase a Bantam book for only 50¢. Here's how!

By ordering any five books at the regular price per order, you can also choose any other single book listed (up to a $4.95 value) for just 50¢. Some restrictions do apply, but for further details why not send for Bantam's listing of titles today!

Just send us your name and address plus 50¢ to defray the postage and handling costs.